ANGELS WATCHING OVER ME

**Center Point
Large Print**

**This Large Print Book carries the
Seal of Approval of N.A.V.H.**

ANGELS WATCHING OVER ME

MICHAEL PHILLIPS

CENTER POINT PUBLISHING
THORNDIKE, MAINE

This Center Point Large Print edition
is published in the year 2004 by arrangement with
Bethany House Publishers.

Copyright © 2003 by Michael Phillips.

Uncle Remus stories are the creation of
Joel Chandler Harris (1848-1908)

The text of this Large Print edition is unabridged.
In other aspects, this book may vary from the original edition.
Printed in Thailand. Set in 16-point Times New Roman type.

ISBN 1-58547-490-8

Library of Congress Cataloging-in-Publication Data

Phillips, Michael R., 1946-
  Angels watching over me / Michael Phillips.--Center Point large print ed.
    p. cm.
  ISBN 1-58547-490-8 (lib. bdg. : alk. paper)
  1. Clairborne, Kathleen (Fictitious character)--Fiction. 2. Jukes, Mary Ann
(Fictitious character)--Fiction. 3. North Carolina--History--Civil War, 1861-1865--Fiction.
4. Female friendship--Fiction. 5. Plantation life--Fiction. 6. Fugitive slaves--Fiction.
7. Race relations--Fiction. 8. Teenage girls--Fiction. 9. Orphans--Fiction. 10. Large type
books. I. Title.

PS3566.H492A85 2004
813'.54--dc22

2004006288

CONTENTS

Katie and I'd been born in the same county only a year apart, but it might as well have been in different centuries on opposite sides of the world. . . .

Remembering . . .

I'VE BEEN MAKING UP STORIES SINCE BEFORE I CAN remember.

As near as I can recollect, it started so as to keep my little brother from crying. If I could just get his attention for a minute or two on something besides the hunger in his stomach or wishing our mama was back in from the fields, he'd shush up and start paying attention. Then I'd have to think up something else mighty quick.

And something after that . . . and I'd string it all together with interesting expressions and in different voices so he'd keep looking at me with those big, wide eyes of his and keep listening and not take to crying again.

Before I knew it, I was spinning out tales that'd keep him quiet for hours. I had no idea what was going to come next but just made it up as I went along. Then the next day when he'd need more stories, I would string along some more where I'd left off.

Sometimes I'd look up, and there'd be our mama,

finally home again and listening too, with a kind of peculiar look on her face to hear what I was telling the young'un, our little Samuel.

"Where'd you hear dat story from, chil'?" she asked me once.

I said I didn't hear it from anyplace. I'd just made it up.

"What 'bout all them little sayin's you add now an' then?"

I shrugged. I hadn't really thought on it.

"Where'd you learn dose?" she pressed.

"No place, Mama," I said.

"But yo're too young ter know sech things."

"I can't help it, Mama. They just come out when I'm tellin' the story."

Then she said something I never forgot, and it's helped me keep my head up through some hard times, and I've had a heap of them.

"Well, chil'," she said, "dis here's a hard life we lead. We neber know what's gwine happen ter any of us from day ter day. You ain't da most fetchin'-lookin' young'un I eber seen. But you got some unordinary smarts in dat brain of yors. So I reckon you'll get along all right fine in dis ole worl', whateber becomes of you."

She paused and smiled at me with that same funny kind of expression on her face. Now that the years have passed and I'm older, I realize it was a look that said how much she loved me. Then she passed the back of her rough black hand across my cheek and spoke again.

"So you jes' keep tellin' yor stories," she said, "an' you pay 'tention to what's in dat head of yors. 'Cause da good Lord's giben you a gif' most folks ain't got."

I nodded, but I only half understood what she was trying to say. It takes a lot of years before young folks can really catch on to what their mamas and papas tell them when they're young.

At first, like I said, I just told stories to my little brother Samuel, and I never had much thought about writing anything down. I loved to listen to the yarns the old slaves would spin around our nightly fires, and I'd tell Sammy those stories too, sometimes adding stuff of my own to them. I especially liked the ones about Mr. Rabbit and Mr. Fox. They were my favorites of the old tales.

I didn't even know how to write when I listened to the first stories and started passing them on to Sammy. But by the time I was ten or so, Mama had taught me to write.

It was uncommon the way she knew how to read and write. Not many slaves had schooling. In fact, lots of their owners got real nervous about slaves learning things like that. But she'd been born to a house slave, and when she was little she listened when the master's children were getting their lessons. She sure didn't get her hands on books too often, but when she did, she ate up the words like she was starving for them.

Anyway, Mama started to bring me every scrap of paper she could find, most of the time taking wrappings from the trash heap and cutting them all down to the same size. Then I started to write things down, kind of like a diary, I reckon. And ideas for made-up stories too. Keeping my diary on those scraps of paper we collected, just like Mama said, helped me through some hard times, and helped me remember things it was important to remember.

So that's how my storytelling all got started. Right now I'm holding a special leather-bound diary in my hands that's nearly as old as I am. How I came to have such a special keepsake is something that's an important part of what I'll be telling you. But for now you should know I've written down things in it from some of those long-ago pieces of paper, and it sure is going to help me remember important events of my life that I want to tell you about.

I've got something else in front of me as I write. It's small and blue and white and gold, but I can't describe it more than that without telling how it came to be, and I'd be getting ahead of myself to do that just yet. But these two things along with my mama's Bible, are all I have left from those days way back then. Putting all those memories into words is going to take every ounce of energy and clear thinking I can muster. So I've got the diary and my memory, such as it is, to help me piece together the events as well as the thoughts, and especially the *feelings,* that shaped my life and Katie's.

Just hang in there with me for a minute, and I'll explain who Katie was.

The particular time I've been talking about, I must have been maybe six or seven, and of course that was before I was writing anything down. My brother was born about three years after me, so that would have made him three or four, which is probably the age when an older sister starts telling a young'un stories.

If that's when I told my first story, that would be more years ago than you likely can imagine, especially some of you who think even thirty or forty is old. I'm not planning to tell you exactly how old I am, but the fact is, I've done a lot of living since my earliest storytelling days.

I remember the first time I ever saw an automobile, and, land's sakes, I was petrified and fascinated all at the same time. When the new century arrived, I was still living in Shenandoah County, and by then it was one thing after another—telephones and cameras and electricity and whatnot—that were all announcing themselves faster than I could catch my breath.

So it's probably not hard to see why I have a difficult time remembering exact dates of things. And if you asked me about any of those stories that I told Samuel, I'd answer that I could no more recall them than I can tell you what happened on the day I was born.

You are probably wondering what has made me want to go back and relive that life back in Shenandoah County, North Carolina. Especially when some of those days were pretty awful. Well, something has happened that will explain why I'm digging around in my past. Mine and Katie's.

But, anyway, I can't quite recollect exactly how all those stories for my little brother got into my head—which ones I heard from other black storytellers and which ones I made up. I think some of them got mixed up with the old slave songs too, because we all loved to sing. And sometimes when I sing those songs now, I seem to be able to recollect things right clearly. But gradually those early years of my life are slowly fading away, kind of like I'm looking off in the distance on a cold, sunny winter morning, when the fog gets thicker and thicker until you can't make out anything at all. That's how it is when I try to think of Samuel now.

Memory's a funny thing. Some bits of it come back easier than others. Sometimes I can remember something that happened when I was seven better than what happened yesterday.

But what I remember most clearly starts when I was fifteen.

That's how old I was when I first laid eyes on Katie.

I can't help thinking of those years, and the changes this world's seen since way back then. That's what folks call nostalgia—recollecting back on times from another era when the world was a different sort of place.

Lots of stories . . . lots of memories come into my mind. Good memories, happy memories. And sad memories too, and some even full of terror, because those were as hard times as anyone would ever want to live through.

I probably told Katie my stories too—at first to keep her mind off being afraid. But I never dreamed the story that folks eventually would ask me about most was my own and Katie's.

It's not just a story. It's what truly happened.

We weren't so very different from any two other girls, except of course that one of us was white and the other colored. And that we lived together through the last part of the War Between the States.

Nowadays I know some folks take offense at calling black folks colored, though I can't myself see what all the fuss is about. I reckon they think it's an insulting word and that we ought to call ourselves black, though I'm not actually black, just a nice dark brown. Yes, I do think of it as "nice." It's how the good Lord made me, and since He is good and He said His creation was good, my skin color must be nice!

Back then we even called each other niggers, though everybody's all up in arms about that word too. Seems a little silly to me. A word is just a word, to my way of thinking. One word's as good—or as bad—as the other. What matters is who you are, not what folks call you. What we lived through back then, Katie and me, was a lot more important than what we were called. No better or no worse than being called "white trash," I suppose.

What I was saying is that because Katie and I were white and black, once we got used to it, the difference between us made us even closer—not because we got to be the same but just because we *were* different. But we were different in more ways than the color of our skin. Something about contrasts makes people stronger, I think. That's sure how it worked in our case.

Years later, when we got older, Katie and I couldn't

even sit together on the train. She sat in front with the white folks, I sat in the colored section. That kind of thing riles a lot of black folks, and I understand that. But for my part, I can't get too upset about it. It's just the way it was. Maybe it shouldn't have been, but it was, and I didn't figure it was my job to fight it. I've got a little different view than most about all that. Laws can be passed to help even things out, but when it all comes down to it, there's only one way for hearts to be changed and real freedom to get around to everybody. In the meantime, I figure it's my job to live my life like the Lord wants me to, not try to set the whole world straight.

Not that I don't think black folks ought to be able to vote and sit where they like and live where they want to and be who they want to be. But if my years on this earth have taught me anything, it's this: the kind of person you are inside is a heap more important in the long run than the rights you have, where you sit, what you're called, and whether you vote.

As I sit here telling our story, or should I say getting ready to start it—though it'll take more than just this first book to get it told, and so far I'm just trying to get my thoughts moving in the right direction—I look down at my wrinkled brown hands on the arms of my chair, and in some ways I can hardly recognize them. These hands of mine have done a lot of things—picking cotton, rocking young'uns, holding a rifle, burying kin.

I reckon the reason I'm telling you all these snippets of my history is to get the idea into your heads that the days I'm going to talk about were a long time ago. But it's not just the kind of time you measure in years. You can't understand my story without realizing how different everything was back then. Like I said, some black folks nowadays get real angry about these rights and those rights, but I doubt most of you younger ones listening to me—or should I say reading this—have any idea how much better you have it. Maybe all this hubbub over rights has to happen, though sometimes it makes me a little uncomfortable. The anger over it all somehow doesn't seem right to me. Everyone in my family was a slave, and I was a slave. And we tried to make the best of it. That's just how it was. Don't get me wrong, I'm not saying slavery ever should have happened. Or that people shouldn't have gone to war abolishing it. But for us back then in Shenandoah County, we just made a life for ourselves in spite of it.

That is, until the year everything changed.

But wait just a minute while I tell you a little bit more about Katie. What I'm fixing to tell isn't really a story at all. It's just who we were, what we did. Katie's life and mine were two streams that ran together and blended eventually into a bigger stream that I guess became a kind of story.

At first whenever we told people about it, Katie and I always described our early years separately, even though the two stories came together soon enough. I started recounting in my own words things I'd heard her tell about first, and then later I started laying it all out through her eyes. So I think what I'm putting down here is one story, a single, unbreakable strand made with two different threads.

For those of you who didn't ever meet Katie, and who may not know me either, my name is Mary Ann Jukes. All my life, folks have just called me Mayme. And Katie was christened Kathleen O'Bannon Clairborne. She was born on a large Southern plantation a few miles west of Greens Crossing, Shenandoah County. I was born on a large Southern plantation a few miles east of Greens Crossing. That's the only part of our beginnings that have much in common.

I'm going to ask you to send your imaginations back a long, long time to when this country fought a war with itself. The year was 1861. That's when Katie always began her part of the story. That's where I'll begin too. Katie was still ten that spring, and I was eleven. But we didn't know each other yet, even though in miles we weren't that far away from each other. But in other ways, we might as well have been on opposite sides of the world.

It all took place northeast of Charlotte, North Carolina, where Shenandoah County and the town of Greens Crossing are located.

WINDS OF CHANGE

1

A HOT SUN ROSE THAT SPRING DAY OVER THE peaceful landscape.

That's how Katie always began to tell it. I reckon the same sun came up and shone down over us both that day, though we were in a different part of the county and all my family were slaves on another plantation six or eight miles away.

The slaves in their quarters, Katie said, looked outside early, saw the heat rising in waves from the damp ground, and sighed.

The fields would be hot, the work hard. The winter had been a mild one, and slave work during those months was more mild too. Today they would feel the beginning of the intense labor that always came at this time of the year. Rolling hills and valleys in that region stretched for hundreds of miles in every direction. Its soil was rich and fertile. In it grew lots of things that brought prosperity to those who owned it.

But it wasn't a very good place or a happy time to be alive if your skin was black. My people knew that as well as the slaves of Katie's father.

He came out from his early breakfast to announce they would complete the ploughing of the eastern fifteen acres today. If the warm weather held after last week's rain, they would move straight to the northern twenty-eight which bordered the river, the master told them. He wanted it ready to plant by next week. The wheat was already in. Now it was time for the cotton.

He returned to the plantation house to finish his breakfast. The male Negroes hitched up the teams, loaded the tools and themselves in three wagons, and set out for the fields. Their women would follow with water and food once the domestic chores were done.

By noon the sun had climbed high, and the damp heat felt more like June than April. No breeze offered relief. Even spring days could get downright uncomfortable in North Carolina, but it was a lot hotter than usual for this early in the season.

A white girl slipped along a wide dirt pathway between two partially cultivated fields. Out of that same dirt her father's cotton crop would be sprouting in white puffy balls four months from now. A golden retriever bounced along at her heels. Rusty had been her constant companion since her father brought him home for her as a pup a year before.

The girl was Kathleen Clairborne. She always told this part of her story as if it were somebody else. She sometimes described it as the time before the person inside her woke up. I reckon everybody's got to come awake sometime. This happens at different times and different ages. Sometimes it's circumstances that wake people up, sometimes pain or hardship. It's an odd thing I've noticed as I've seen more of life—happiness alone doesn't usually do much to help folks wake up on the inside. What wakes people up the quickest is some kind of tragedy or grief. Most of the time, I suppose, it's just getting older and starting to *think*.

It's sad, though, that some people never do seem to come all the way awake no matter how long they live.

But as Katie looked back later on the little girl walking in the fields, she said it felt like she was a different person then. She hadn't come awake yet.

She had as few worries in the world as a girl can have. Her carefree gait suited this kind of a Saturday. She understood as little about cotton, which the black people were digging the earth to make ready to grow, as she did about the growing season. Neither was she aware of the great amount of slave labor required to make a plantation owner such as her father a wealthy man. Katie wore nice frocks decorated with ribbon and lace and played with expensive dolls that came from places like England or France. But she had never given any thought to why she had them. Her life was full of music and books and pretty things.

Nothing particular had driven her outside that Saturday morning. Her actions, Katie said later, were guided by impulse, not decision. She had tired of playing inside and now simply found herself moving along the road eastward away from the house with one of those dolls under her arm. She had not *decided* to go for a walk. She just found herself doing so. Katie did what came into her head and took what happened in life, without wondering where it came from or why.

Flies buzzed about, and bees busily conducted their springtime business, and they had plenty to do because there were wild flowers blooming all across the moist, green, humid countryside. In the heat, Katie had slowed her movements to a lazy stroll. Even Rusty had decided to save his energy and simply sniffed at the grass on each side of the path.

I can still smell the land on a day like that. There's nothing like the moist earth in the South after a spring rain. Now and then the distant low of a cow could be heard as Katie walked along, though in the heat, even their *moos* sounded weary. A thin haze lay over the hills in the distance, as it usually did. The earth and its inhabitants were alive with growth and activity. Yet at the same time a sleepy tranquility hung over the land, subdued under the smokelike mist clinging to the mountains in the west.

More changes were in the air, however, than Katie or her father, or than I or my family where we lived, or than *anybody* realized. New breezes were blowing—that's how Katie used to describe it. But the slaves with sweat pouring off their black foreheads in Shenandoah County northeast of Charlotte, between the Piedmont Plateau and the Blue Ridge Mountains, they couldn't yet feel them either.

They would feel them soon enough. So would Katie. So would I.

Four years later, destiny would bring us together. When that time came, cruelty and terror would be carried on those winds of change. For many in both races, the storm would bring heartache and destruction. Lots of good folks would die for the cause that both North and South called freedom. Others would learn to grow strong, though it wouldn't be easy, and that kind of inner strength would cost them many tears.

But most people alive in 1861 knew nothing of the significance of the times, or realized that history was about to be made. Or that they would be part of it.

Kathleen O'Bannon Clairborne didn't know it. Neither did Mary Ann Jukes.

We were both oblivious to the fact that we were living in a newly created nation calling itself the Confederate States of America. We had not heard of Fort Sumter, almost two hundred miles southeast on the South Carolina coast, where troops were already gathering to defend the right of those Southern states to maintain their independence.

And so Katie went on with her life as she always had. The slaves did their work and she played with her dolls.

But winds of change were in the air. Folks would have no choice but to come awake eventually.

Even two little girls.

SPECIAL PLACE

2

M O'NIN' TO YA, MIZ KATHLEEN," CALLED OUT A colored woman as Katie walked by. Katie glanced toward the workers and smiled.

The large woman was carrying a bucket of water to the field where the men were digging and hoeing. She was as little aware of events about to engulf her as the daughter of the plantation master who owned her. The slave woman had heard bits and pieces about Abraham Lincoln and Jefferson Davis, who had become presidents of their two countries a few months earlier. But if someone had told her that a year and a half later the man called Lincoln would issue a proclamation declaring that she, her husband Mathias, and their three children were free, she would no more have been able to grasp it than to think the sun would not rise tomorrow.

White and black alike through the South were steeped in the tradition of their cultures. Change was not something they were expecting. But both Katie and the slave woman would have to get used to it eventually. For by now the events bringing change to their lives could not be stopped.

Katie continued past the toiling Negroes. Another dirt path intersected with the one she was on. She took it to the left, and gradually realized she had come around to the opposite side of the field.

She stopped and gazed across it. Yes, this was the same field. She had never gone this way before, but she recognized the woods just beyond. Books and music, like I said, were her usual companions. But recently she had discovered a special place, and she had made friends with nature.

She left the road and entered a large grassy field. By and by she found herself walking through scattered pines at its far side, coming a few minutes later to the brook which wound through the wood. A small pond lay at the center of a tiny secluded meadow, and then the brook flowed out again at the other side.

This was her own private place. No one else in the whole world, or so Katie thought, knew of it. Katie had learned to love animals, beginning with her beloved Rusty, and now she talked to squirrels and brought them things to eat. She always told Rusty to sit down and behave himself so the other animals wouldn't be afraid. And even though he was only a year old and full of a pup's energy, he seemed to sense what she meant and always quieted when she came here.

There were fish in the pond. Deer came to drink from its edge. Both had become her friends. The fish didn't know it. But the deer did. And gradually they had grown used to the small girl's presence. They were not afraid to drink when she was here.

Katie knew the birds too, and two gray rabbits that lived in a nearby thicket. She saw a raccoon once. But coons didn't usually come during the day, and try as she might to come early in the morning and sit as still as a rock, the one she had seen never returned. There was also a turtle that sometimes swam about in the water.

I wish you could hear Katie describe her special place in her own words. Katie was as much a poet in her own way as I am a storyteller. She wrote many poems, though she kept them mostly to herself. Her mother read to her a lot and taught her to play the piano and violin. I think people who can make music can also make words into music. Maybe that's what poems are—musical words.

I believe the feelings and observations that later came out in her poems must have been inside her way back when she was just a little girl. I'm sure it takes a long time to make a poet, with things going deep and taking root in the subconscious. It must take years for fancies to get nourished in the soil of imagination before they're able to come out in actual words. Some of you probably know what I mean, because I'm sure some of you have written poems too. I could never write a poem, but watching Katie helped me understand it a little better. She was always observing, taking things in, living in her imagination, and like I said, *feeling* things more deeply than she let on, deeper than a practical person like me felt them. Maybe she felt things deeper than she even realized herself.

So I like to think of Katie sitting by the pond in the woods watching for animals, not necessarily thinking about what was going on around her but *feeling* it, with the invisible music of poetry moving silently inside her even before she wrote her first poem.

If she had known about praying then, she might have called such times praying. Some folks think praying happens only when you're in church or are actually talking to God. But I'm not so sure. I think that when you're feeling the silent mysteries of the world, and feeling the tunes that God put into it for us to listen to, and when you let His creation make you happy, then that's a kind of praying too. But that's just one old black lady's opinion on the matter.

One thing I do know, whether you call Katie's times in the woods beside the pond praying or not, she was learning to feel a love for the world around her that eventually made her able both to pray and write poems expressing what she felt inside.

I've always been thankful for this quiet side of Katie, because there came a time in my life when it would teach me a lot and make a better person of me.

Listening to Katie tell about the trees and fields and the animals made you think you were there. I could smell the scent that the sun drew out of the pine trees when she was talking about it.

On this day she set her doll—I think she was named Rebecca—down beside her as she sat on her favorite rock, then picked up a stick and began jabbing at a few pebbles and flicking them toward the water's edge. All the while she was looking around at everything about her. And though she might not have said it in these words, I think her heart was glad to be alive.

A Visit to Town

3

THE SUN DAWNED JUST AS IT HAD MANY TIMES before during Kathleen Clairborne's young life.

She rolled over in bed to see its light slanting through her window. She gave a sleepy sigh of pleasure. It was Monday and no more rain was in sight. They would be able to go into town. Her mother had promised her a new dress for her birthday, but Katie had been afraid more rain might cancel the outing. Greens Crossing was six miles away. It was not a trip her mother made often, especially if the road was muddy.

There was not anything unusual about this particular day. The sun had beamed into Katie's window on countless mornings just like it. Yet this would not be like any of those other days.

Katie would look back on this as the day when, for her, everything began to change.

Greens Crossing was not a large town. A handful of stores, a livery stable, a school, a church, a bank, a general store and post office, and one saloon clustered together at the intersection of two roads. We lived a little closer to town than she did, but I'd never set foot in it in my life.

Though the Clairbornes' Rosewood was not the

largest plantation of the region, they were known by most of the citizens of Greens Crossing. Richard Clairborne, Katie's father, was a hard worker, fair to his slaves, faithful to his family, but a man who kept mostly to himself. He didn't have close friends in town. His three sons were like him in that way. Neither they nor Katie attended the Greens Crossing school. The Clairbornes weren't seen at church except for occasional special circumstances. Six miles is a fair piece by horse and buggy.

Once or twice a year, Mrs. Clairborne rode the even more daunting nineteen miles into Charlotte. That's where she bought her own clothes and Katie's and did most of the family's shopping. But Katie had grown two inches over the winter, and the dressmaker in Greens Crossing was as skilled as any in the city. Since it would not be until later in the summer that she and her husband would be taking a wagon into Charlotte again, the buggy would carry them into Greens Crossing today.

Katie and her mother left the dressmaker's an hour after arriving in town and stepped from the wooden sidewalk to cross the dirt street.

"Hello, Rosalind," a woman's voice called out behind them.

Mrs. Clairborne paused and turned toward the general store owner's wife, who had spoken to her. Katie continued into the street, still thinking of the soft, pretty fabric they had picked out and the bright yellow hat they had ordered to go with the new dress. She didn't notice her mother stopping to chat with Mrs.

27

Hammond. Neither did she see two riders suddenly gallop recklessly around the saloon at the corner.

A tumult of shouts and whinnies suddenly filled the air.

"Get outta the way, you—!"

Mrs. Clairborne swiftly turned toward the ruckus.

"Katie . . . watch out!" she cried as she ran frantically toward the street.

Suddenly a man's heavy step ran past Mrs. Clairborne. The next instant Katie was thrown to the ground. A second later the riders thundered by.

The tall, lanky Negro picked himself up off the ground beside the frightened girl. He stooped down, took her hand, and pulled Katie to her feet.

"Yo needs be a mite mo careful crossin' da street, Miss Kat'leen," he said, brushing the dirt from his trousers and shirt. "Dem two soldiers mighta run right ober da top er you."

Mrs. Clairborne rushed toward them.

"Oh, Henry, I can't thank you enough!" she exclaimed to the black man who worked in the livery stable. "Katie, are you all right?" she said, taking Katie's hand. Still too stunned to speak, Katie nodded.

"Dern blamed soldiers," muttered Henry, who had bought his own freedom some years before, "dey been raisin' a ruckus roun' 'bout fo days now. Ah doan know what's goin' on. De're all ridin' down t' Charleston. Somethin's up fo sho—I been hearin' talk 'bout an army gatherin'. Yor husband joinin', ma'am?"

"I don't know, Henry," sighed Mrs. Clairborne. "I

really don't know."

As they talked, Katie gazed up into the face of the tall man. The shine in his eyes and the gleam of his perfect teeth drew her gaze into his earnest countenance. An uncommon sensation of gratitude welled up within the heart of the young white girl for the Negro man who had run in front of racing horses' hooves to keep her from being trampled.

Mrs. Clairborne's voice intruded abruptly into Katie's reflections.

"Kathleen, sometimes I wonder if there's a brain in that head of yours," she said, pulling on Katie's hand as they walked away. "What gets into you to wander into the street like that?"

"Ah wouldn't be too hard on da chil', ma'am," said Henry from behind them.

"I'm grateful for what you've done, Henry," rejoined Mrs. Clairborne, turning back toward the stable hand, "but now you must really mind your own business. The child is careless and scatterbrained. She needs to watch where she is going."

"Yes'm," said the black man. He tipped his hat to mother and daughter, then ambled back in the direction of the livery.

PUZZLING WORDS

4

AN HOUR OR TWO AFTER FALLING ASLEEP THAT SAME night, Katie awoke to voices coming from downstairs. She recognized her mother and father talking in hushed tones, not wanting Katie or her older brothers to hear. They weren't exactly arguing, but her father sounded urgent and determined, her mother tense and afraid.

Strange and undefined fears filled Katie's heart as she lay awake and strained to listen. She tiptoed toward her door.

"Don't you understand, Rosalind?" her father was saying. "I have to go. If we don't fight, everything we have lived for will be taken away."

"Why does it have to be you?" implored her mother.

"What would you have me do, stay home when the rest of North Carolina's men are risking their lives for our freedom? I won't spend my life thinking I was a coward."

"But the boys, Richard, surely they don't have to—"

"We will be back in a few months, Rosalind. It won't take longer than that."

"I can understand Joseph," Katie heard her begin again. "But the others are so—"

"Caleb and Jason want to go," he interrupted. "I'm

not going to stop them. They're men now too."

"Sixteen and seventeen—that's hardly men."

"You can't keep them boys forever, Rosalind."

It was quiet for a few long seconds. Not wanting to hear her parents argue but unable to prevent herself from eavesdropping, Katie put her ear closer to the opening.

"Where will you be—will I be able to get in touch with you?" she heard her mother finally say. Her voice was soft and hesitant. Katie could tell her mother was starting to cry.

"I'll be moving about," answered her father. "Fort Sumter at first, then I don't know. It depends on how long it takes us to drive the Yankees back north. You'll just have to take care of things."

"What if your brother . . . what if Burchard makes trouble with you gone?"

"There's no reason for him to find out."

"He always seems to know what you do, almost before you do it."

"He'll be busy with his own crops now that spring's come. I doubt you'll even see him before I'm back."

"What if I do?"

"He can't do anything legally in the short time I'm away. You'll be fine, Rosalind."

"What about the plantation . . . the crops?"

"Everything will be all right for a few months. The winter wheat's in, the new wheat's planted. The cotton will be in within two weeks. The boys and I will be back in time to harvest."

"What if you're . . . you're delayed?"

Katie could feel the shakiness in her mother's voice. By now her mother was crying in earnest. It filled Katie with a kind of fear she had never known before. Her mother was the focal point for everything in life—a rock, strength itself. Her mother knew everything and could do anything. To hear her cry seemed to unravel the very fabric of her existence. Katie would not have put it into those kind of words back when she was a child. But as she stood trembling, she felt dreadful forebodings. She had never heard her mother sound this way, so uncertain, so afraid. She had never heard her mother weep.

But then her father's voice again floated up into her hearing.

"The slaves know what to do," he was saying. "They just need someone to push them, to crack the whip every day or two. Tell Mathias what to do. He's a good man. He'll keep the darkies in line and take care of the crops."

"How will I know what to tell him?"

"Just tell him to get the cotton planted and then keep it weeded. And Leroy knows more about animals than any darkie alive. Just tell them to run things for a while—we'll be back by fall."

"What about the grain?"

"Let the wheat turn golden, then give it another week before the scythe is put to it. The color's the key—green's got to be gone and the head gold. But if you see rain coming, get it in even if it hasn't been a week. Once it's gold, you've got to get the wheat under the roof before the rains come, else it'll fall and rot on the ground. But Mathias knows all that. He and Leroy know what to do. Just make sure it's gold."

Their voices grew soft.

". . . what about . . . and if my brother . . ."

Her mother's voice drifted and she couldn't hear the rest. Now her father spoke again.

". . . hasn't come around in all this time . . ."

". . . but if he comes around again . . . his gold . . . what if he . . ."

". . . not going to show up with a war on . . . give it to him like you always said . . . but probably back in California . . . for all we know."

". . . hate to think . . . if Templeton found out . . . you not here . . ."

". . . couldn't possibly . . . unless . . . your family . . ."

". . . been too long . . . my family . . ."

". . . sister might know where . . ."

". . . got it out of Ward . . . hate each other too much . . . Ward would never give him . . ."

". . . always ran with a rough bunch . . . tell him . . . haven't seen him in years . . ."

". . . what should I . . ."

". . . just keep . . . down where . . ."

Again her father's and mother's voices became so distant that Katie could make out no more of their conversation. She crept back into her bed. But she couldn't go to sleep. She lay for a long time confused and afraid.

What did her mother's two brothers have to do with whether the wheat was ripe and golden? She'd never even seen either of them, though she'd heard her parents talk about them before. She knew her father didn't like either of them.

Talk of war, talk of her father and brothers leaving—it all frightened her.

But gradually she fell asleep and dreamed of golden fields of wheat, of golden coins, and the light golden hair of her doll Rebecca. . . .

Only a few days later Katie's father and three older brothers rode away from Rosewood, leaving the plantation in the hands of Katie's mother and the slaves. The conflict forever known as the War Between the States had arrived . . . and life in North Carolina would never be the same again.

WAR COMES

5

K ATIE KNEW HER FATHER OWNED SLAVES, BUT LIKE most young white children—and I suppose black ones like me too—she took it all as part of the natural order of things. She'd never thought about it, never questioned it, never stopped to wonder whether it was right or wrong. She had no idea what the conflict between North and South was all about.

The fighting broke out on April 12 of 1861 when Confederate soldiers attacked Fort Sumter in the Charleston harbor. The Union commander of the fort surrendered two days later. The war had begun.

In July the Union army was routed at Manassas in Virginia. It looked like the prediction of Katie's father might come true, that the South would defeat the North in plenty of time for them to get home for the harvest.

But when Katie and her mother next saw Richard Clairborne a few weeks later, he didn't have the joy of victory on his face. He had come home to tell them that Katie's brother Jason had been killed in the battle. Her other two brothers were off somewhere with the army. He didn't know when he'd see either of them again.

Katie's mother cried for days. By the time she said good-bye to her husband a second time, hard lines of grief had already begun to etch themselves onto her face. Despite her husband's optimistic words, she was well aware that the war could take the lives of her other sons too, as well as make a widow of her. She did not cry or argue at his departure this time. She was too angry to cry—angry at her husband for getting involved, angry at Abraham Lincoln, angry at Jefferson Davis, angry at them all. Why did men always have to fight? Couldn't they see the stupidity and senselessness of it?

With steely eyes she watched him ride off without answers to the questions that had plagued women like her for untold centuries. She loved him. But at that moment she thought Richard Clairborne to be about the most stupid man alive. He was leaving his wife and daughter alone just so he could try to kill other men who had also left wives and daughters behind at their homes. Possibly he would get himself killed by one of those men. Men killing other men . . . and for what?

She shook her head and turned back into the house. Matthias or not, there was work to do, and it was going to be hard and would test every bone in her body. She knew that well enough by now. If men like her husband thought the war didn't really matter to the women at home, then they were fools.

She couldn't have been more right. When it came, the war came to everyone.

The fighting dragged on much longer than Richard Clairborne or most Southerners had figured it would. But Katie's mother was not surprised. She had seen it coming. And she knew it would get worse. Rosalind Clairborne did her best to hold everything at Rose-wood together, but daily the hardships increased.

Especially for rich folks like the Clairbornes, who had been insulated from the harsh realities of life, the difficulties of the war spread like a creeping rot. At first everything on the plantation continued pretty much the same. But without the master and his sons overseeing the slaves, they gradually slacked off, working at a slower pace and accomplishing less. Even Mathias, who had always been as faithful as any black man could be to his master, couldn't keep the lethargy from setting in.

The first year's wheat eventually got harvested and sold, and the cotton crop was about normal. When Mrs. Clairborne and Mathias and Jeremiah took the three loaded wagons of harvested cotton into Mr. Watson's mill, the money for it was good enough to keep the Clairborne account at the Shenandoah bank full for another year, feeding Katie and her mother, along with the slaves, and providing for some winter repairs about the place. They had most everything they needed.

But by the following year, Rosalind Clairborne was beginning to see inevitable signs that the work was falling behind. The crops were slow getting sown, and as the summer progressed the fields weren't as well attended. Fences were starting to require attention, and more than once she had to run through the fields herself to chase away deer nibbling at the shoots of wheat. Sometimes Leroy was late to milk the cows. And she even had to watch Beulah and Elvia a little more carefully with the kitchen and household chores—something she had never had to do before. A drought through most of July didn't help matters. As a result, the year's crop was less than half as plentiful as the previous year, and Katie's mother was feeling the financial pinch. She knew the plantation was suffering. One of the wagons was old, and her husband had talked of buying a new one this year. But now she wouldn't be able to do so. And throughout the previous winter they had to slaughter more cattle, chickens, and hogs than she would have liked just to feed themselves and the slaves. They couldn't continue this way or the stock would eventually dwindle down to nothing.

It was during that second year that she was forced to

start borrowing from the bank. As she did, she silently railed at both her husband and her brother, the one for putting her in this position, the other for having the means to help but being so irresponsible that he had disappeared without a trace. She ought to just—

No, she said to herself. Things hadn't gotten quite that bad yet, and she would pay off the bank with the next year's crops.

Mrs. Clairborne was forced to understand much that she'd heard from her husband for years, and realize why he'd complained about the slaves, the weather, the fences, the constant drain of cash, and a hundred other things. And always more bills appeared than she could manage—where did they all come from? It wasn't easy managing a plantation, she had heard him say many times. Now that she had to do it for herself, Rosalind Clairborne realized just how hard it really was.

She vowed that she would roll up her sleeves and go down to the slave quarters every day and get the work started herself. She would supervise them throughout the day too. How many times had she heard her husband say, "If you don't stand over their shoulders and make them do what you tell them, nothing will get done."

She had been lax. She had assumed everyone would do just as she said. A lot of what had happened this last season was her own fault. From now on she would watch things more closely, even if it meant getting out in the fields every day and working right along with them. If that's what it took to keep the cotton hoed and free of weeds, that's what she would do.

She would make them work. If her husband could do it, she could. She couldn't afford another bad year.

It was a bewildering and lonely time in Katie's life. At one time she came upon her mother, uncharacteristically exasperated with Beulah or Elvia, another time just sitting and crying from sheer exhaustion. Yet her mother's attempted explanations made little sense in Katie's ears.

And Mrs. Clairborne's irritation with Katie's innocence occasionally boiled over.

Katie was out next to the pasture one day, playing with a doll and talking to a cow grazing on the other side of the fence. Rusty lay curled up asleep at her side. Mrs. Clairborne hurried up to them.

"Kathleen, what are you doing!" exclaimed her mother in frustration. "Do I have to do everything around here myself? What am I going to do with you if you're always in your own little dreamworld?"

Katie was confused at her mother's outburst.

"The dream is over, Kathleen," Mrs. Clairborne went on, hands on her hips. "You're going to have to be in charge of your own home someday. It's time you learned to do some things. And I need help around here. So we're going to start right now. I'm going to teach you to handle a team of horses. It will be a big help to me if you can go down to the slave quarters with a wagon of food now and then. Come with me while I hitch up the horses."

Katie complied and learned to do whatever she was told, though at the end of this day, when the lesson with the team and wagon was done, she went to her room, sat down with Rebecca and Peg and Sarah in her lap, and started to cry.

Why was her mother so irritable? Why had she said those things today?

Her mother never read to her now, and hardly ever smiled. There used to be music in the house all the time, and they used to go to concerts. The war had made everything so dreary. She didn't feel like playing her violin or the piano all by herself, and her mother never sat down at the piano anymore either.

TWISTER

6

ROSALIND CLAIRBORNE READ ABOUT MR. LINCOLN'S Emancipation Proclamation in the Greens Crossing *Clarion* in January of 1863, and it didn't help matters for her. Though only a few of the Rosewood slaves knew how to read, and they never got their hands on a newspaper, somehow they learned of the proclamation within a few weeks. How news traveled so fast among slaves was a mystery to Katie's mother.

But soon enough she saw signs that they had heard about it and were wondering what it was going to mean in their lives. After that it became yet more difficult to get the work of the plantation done.

All through the South, colored folk were restless. And white plantation owners were nervous.

By now Katie was getting to an age where she could be of some actual help with the chores around the house. She still could be distracted with daydreams, but for the first time in her life Katie's white cheeks were often stained with dirt and her dainty hands wore blisters. With money scarce, there were no more pretty dresses or new dolls.

Another year went by.

Things on the plantation did not improve. Still the war dragged on. Rosalind had heard nothing from her husband for over six months when a brief hurried note was passed along to her from a wounded soldier returning home. Mr. Clairborne was still alive—at least he was then.

In the fall a rare tornado swept through North Carolina.

As the day progressed and the wind rose into a howling frenzy, Katie's mother kept close watch on the dark horizon. Finally the wind whipped into such a fury she wondered that the roof didn't blow off. Then she saw the shape of the wind funnel. It appeared out of nowhere. Suddenly there it was just a few miles away!

"Elvia!" she cried to the Negro cook, who was younger and about half the size of Beulah. "Run to the slave quarters and tell everyone to hurry up here as fast as they can."

"But, Miz Clair—"

"Now, Elvia! Run as fast as you can. There's a twister coming. Everyone—especially the little ones . . . hurry!"

The eyes of the terrified woman were now as big as two white saucers in the middle of her brown face. Finally grasping the urgency of her mistress's command, she turned and left the kitchen at a run.

Mrs. Clairborne yelled for Katie, then ran to the middle of the parlor, pulled back the rug, and opened the hinged door in the floor that led to the underground cellar. She didn't stop to wonder what her husband would do in this situation. There'd never been a tornado this close before. She knew it wasn't proper to bring any but house slaves inside. None of them but Beulah and Elvia had ever set foot in the plantation house.

But she couldn't worry about that now. She'd think about the right and wrong of it later. If her husband was angry that black folks had come into his home, so be it. Right now she had to find a way to keep them all alive.

But before they came to safety she had to make sure they saw nothing that shouldn't be seen. She hurried down the narrow stairs.

"Mama," she heard a voice through the trapdoor a few moments later.

"I'm down in the cellar, Kathleen," she called. "Come down the ladder."

"May I bring my doll?"

"Yes, Katie—just hurry."

While Katie climbed down, her mother finished her business.

"Wait for me here, Kathleen," she said as soon as Katie reached the bottom. "I've got to run back upstairs and bring Beulah and the others down. I'll be back soon."

"What about Rusty?"

"Rusty will have to take care of himself."

By the time Mrs. Clairborne reached the kitchen again and looked out the window with Beulah at her side, already she saw a line of black folks running toward the house, some of the women carrying babies, the men hurrying them along as fast as they could. Behind them, the black twister was maybe only two miles away, close enough that she could see the swirling wind whipping up bushes and small trees and debris inside it.

"Hurry . . . into the house, all of you," she cried. "Beulah—show them where to go!"

In ones and twos they ran inside, hardly thinking what they were doing. A few paused long enough to wipe their feet. But they were quickly interrupted by their master's wife.

"Don't worry about the dirt, Jeremiah—just get into the cellar . . . Jeb . . . Mathias—come everyone, hurry!"

Minutes later Katie's mother let the trapdoor down to the living room floor from the bottom and climbed down the narrow stairs to join the others all huddled together on the floor. A lone candle flickered in the darkness.

Then they waited, listening. Someone started to pray, and others joined in. Beulah hummed a few bars of a song, then the group began singing, "All night, all day . . . angels watching over me. . . ."

The wind could be heard faintly moaning up the stairs. Mrs. Clairborne knew if the tornado came close enough to take their house, they would hear a roar louder than any wind they could imagine. But she heard nothing like that. Gradually the moaning and whistling sounds above them died away.

After a few minutes, she rose, crept up the stairs, and lifted the trapdoor a crack.

The air was still. She lifted it the rest of the way and climbed up. The house was just as they had left it. She clasped trembling hands together and whispered, "Thank you, Lord."

"It's passed," she said into the cellar. "You can come out."

Slowly the slaves made their way up the ladder, now pausing to look around them at the rich furnishings and huge fancy house where the master and his family lived. Silently they all filed outside and back to the shacks that were their homes.

"Mathias," Mrs. Clairborne instructed as they left, "give me a report on the damage, will you?"

"Yes'm," replied the black man as he walked away.

He returned an hour later with the news, which wasn't nearly as bad as it could have been. The roof of one of the slave buildings had been blown off, he said. A path had been torn through the wheat, ruining about a third of the crop. A couple of trees were down. And two sections of fence had been ripped into kindling.

Mrs. Clairborne took in the report with relief.

"Well, see to it all, Mathias," she said.

"Yes'm."

"The roof first of all, then the fences."

A VISITOR

7

IN JULY OF 1864 MRS. CLAIRBORNE WAS WORKING IN one of the nearby fields with a handful of Negroes, ones who had not drifted away from the plantation to find better situations in the North. They were hoeing weeds from between long rows of cotton. She was hot and tired, and her dress was stained with sweat and dust. The barking of dogs in the distance intruded into the sounds of their labor.

She paused and looked toward the house. A man was riding toward it on horseback. Her eyes squinted and she muttered under her breath.

"I am afraid I have a visitor," she said. "Mathias, once this field is done, have the men start on the twelve acres on the other side of the creek."

"Yes'm," replied the black man without glancing up.

"And I would like you to go check on that broken door on the barn, and the smokehouse has a leak somewhere in the roof," she added.

"Yes, Miz Clairborne."

She set down her hoe and walked across the field in

the direction of the house. Her visitor saw her approaching, dismounted, tied his reins to the hitching rail, and stood waiting with an amused grin on his face.

"Keeping the darkies company in the fields, eh, Rosalind?" he remarked, arching a brow as she walked toward him.

"Hello, Templeton," she replied, ignoring the remark. "I didn't expect to see you here with a war on," she added testily.

"I try to avoid the war whenever possible," he said with a confident smile.

"You appear to be succeeding. From the looks of it, I would say the hostilities have not hampered your style," she went on with sarcasm. "I am surprised to see you so far south. I assume you are not taking up the Union cause?"

"My only cause is . . ." He hesitated.

"Yourself?" she said. "You don't need to pretend to be other than what you are around me. I know you too well."

He threw back his head and laughed. "I'm not sure how to take that, Rosalind."

"Take it any way you like," she rejoined as they walked toward the house. "What are you doing here?"

"Aren't you at least going to offer me a cup of coffee?"

"We haven't had coffee in this house for months," Rosalind retorted.

From her room upstairs, Katie heard a man's voice coming from below. Thinking her father had come home, she ran downstairs into the kitchen. There she saw a strange man in fancy clothes talking to her mother. Disappointed, she paused in the doorway.

"Ah," the man said, glancing toward her, "this must be little Kathleen."

"Yes, sir," said Katie, hesitating momentarily, then moving toward her mother.

"Kathleen, this is your uncle . . . Mr. Daniels," she said slowly, sounding almost reluctant to make the introduction.

As Katie stared at the man she did not remember seeing before, she wondered how he managed to keep so clean. His black suit and vest showed not a speck of lint or the slightest wrinkle. The ruffled white shirt inside it sparkled with pearl studs down the center, matching the cufflinks that showed at his wrists beneath the sleeves of his coat. He held a black wide-brimmed hat in hands that weren't half so rough as her mother's, and looked too white and soft for a man's. She could not keep her eyes from drifting back and forth from his thin black mustache to the ruffles and pearl studs on his shirt.

"How do you do, Kathleen," responded the man with a smile that showed perfect white teeth. "You may call me Uncle Templeton. How would you like a sweet piece of hard candy?"

"Keep your candy to yourself, Templeton," interjected Katie's mother.

"Come on, sis, one piece of candy won't hurt her . . . will it, Kathleen?" he added, flashing another grin and brief wink in Katie's direction.

"You're treating her like a child."

"How old are you, Kathleen?"

"Fourteen, sir."

"Ah, I see what your mother means—why, you're practically a grown lady. Come over here . . . I always carry a few sweets in my pocket. Come and see if you can find one."

Mrs. Clairborne put a kettle of water on the stove for tea, watching with obvious annoyance as Katie took her uncle's bait and slowly approached. She had seen the enterprising glint in his eye, as well as his smooth talk and clever words too many times to trust him for two minutes, even with his own niece.

"Templeton, leave her alone," she said as she returned to the table.

"I mean the girl no harm, Rosalind. I only want to give her a piece of candy."

"Why? Once you get whatever it is you want from me, you'll be gone. Trying to win Katie over wouldn't make me give you so much as a dime, if I had one."

The man turned to Katie with an injured expression.

"Kathleen, what's my sister talking about?" he said in a hurt tone. "You don't think there's anything wrong with my giving you a little piece of candy, do you?"

Katie stared at him with big eyes but didn't answer. Her uncle now turned back toward her mother.

"Come on, sis—let me see a smile. You've been working too hard. I saw that the moment I rode up. If you'll give your brother a smile, maybe I'll give you a piece of candy too."

He turned his chair and moved it a little closer to Katie, now holding out one of his hands to draw her toward him.

"You know, Kathleen," he said in a soft, confidential voice, "when she was your age, your mother was about the prettiest girl in all Philadelphia. She was just as pretty as you are. Once when she was sixteen I brought her a lovely gown from New York. My . . . you should have seen her! When she put on that dress, every young man for miles around wanted to dance with Rosalind Daniels."

"Stop it, Templeton," Mrs. Clairborne objected, though unable to keep from laughing lightly. "Now you're telling Katie stories."

"Why, your mother," Daniels went on as if he had not heard her, "might have been the prettiest girl, not just in the county, but in all the North."

As he spoke, Katie's uncle now cut a glance toward his sister out of the corner of one eye. He could tell Rosalind's defenses were starting to break down under his charm, just as they always did.

The hint of a smile cracked her lips. "Well, give Katie the candy," she said, "and then you might as well bring in your things, if you've got any, and unsaddle your horse. It's too late to move on, so you might as well spend the night with us and get some warm food inside you."

"Thank you, Rosalind," said Daniels, releasing Katie's hand and leaning back in the chair. He opened his pocket toward Katie so she could put her hand inside it. "That's right hospitable of you."

"All right now, Kathleen," said her mother when Katie had found a piece of candy and began unwrapping the paper around it, "why don't you go back up to your room so your uncle and I can talk."

"Yes, ma'am. Thank you for the candy, sir," she added, smiling at her uncle.

It did not take long for Mrs. Clairborne's suspicious mood to return. As Katie walked slowly through the parlor toward the stairs, their voices picked up the conversation.

"I'm asking you again," said her mother, "—what are you doing here, Templeton?"

"Looks like you could use a man's help around the place," her uncle drawled. "Where are all the slaves? You used to have a real nice-looking young house slave . . . what was her name?"

Katie went into her room, but the voices from below continued to drift up into her hearing.

The kitchen held a long, uncomfortable silence. Mrs. Clairborne stared at her brother for several seconds, daggers in her eyes.

"You remember her name well enough," she finally said. "She's gone." She paused, then added, "They're mostly all gone now."

Her brother took in the information with pretended disinterest, then tried to laugh it off lightly. "Well, I still say you could use a man's help around here," he said. "Look at your hands, all blistered up. And I hate to say it, but I've known ladies who smelled better, Rosalind."

"Never you mind what I smell like," Rosalind said.

"I've got work to do, and a little honest sweat never hurt a woman any more than it hurt a man. But you're right, I could use a man—a man who knows how to dirty his hands and work, something I don't think you know anything about."

"Is that any way to talk to your older brother?"

"I never see you unless one of your schemes goes sour and you want something from me. Well, we've got no money this time, Templeton. Whatever I have I owe the bank. I've already had to borrow twice. So if you're looking for a stake in a poker game or some other scheme—"

"You've got me all wrong, my dear. I wouldn't come just to weasel money out of you."

"You've done it enough times before. I'd have thought you'd got enough when Father died to last a lifetime. But it was gone in . . . what—a year?"

"Two, actually," he replied, a grin rather than remorse on his face.

The kitchen was quiet again for a few seconds.

"Have you seen Ward?" asked Daniels after a moment.

"What could you possibly want with him?" asked Mrs. Clairborne. "You and your brother haven't spoken in years."

"Maybe we've had a reconciliation."

"I'll believe that when I see it. You and Ward were always at each other's throats, both of you squandering what was given you, then trying to get rich without working for it."

"That's Ward, all right," laughed Daniels.

"Well, I haven't seen him for years," said Katie's mother, getting up from the table and walking to the stove to check the kettle.

"I heard he came by here after he got back from California," her brother probed further.

"Yes, he came by," she nodded.

"When?"

"I don't know—a year or two before the war broke out. He was gone just as suddenly as he came, and I haven't seen him since."

"He give you anything?" The question sounded casual.

"No . . . what do you mean?" she answered a little hesitantly. "He didn't give me anything," she added more forcefully.

"Word around was that he struck it rich out West."

"Word going around where? With whom?"

"Friends of his."

"Well, I know nothing about what happened when he was in California, or what he's been doing since. For all I know he might be dead by now."

Rosalind busied herself at the stove.

"Maybe I'll just stick around for a spell," said Daniels after a few long seconds. "Who knows, maybe the country life will suit me."

"I invited you to spend the night and have a meal or two with us, not stay for a spell."

"You wouldn't put your poor brother out with a war on, would you?"

"You just better be gone when Richard comes home."

Templeton Daniels and Richard Clairborne had never hit it off any more than he and Ward. Without responding, he slowly rose from the table.

"I think I'll do what you say and go take care of my horse while you're fixing me that tea," he said.

Rosalind watched him leave the house and shook her head. She knew as well as her brother that there was nothing she could do to get rid of him until he was good and ready to go. He had always done whatever he wanted without worrying about how it affected anyone else. It didn't appear he was going to change his ways anytime soon.

A WEEK LATER, Katie awoke early and came downstairs on her way outside to the outhouse. She walked into the kitchen to see her uncle rummaging through the cupboards. He spun around at the sound of her footsteps.

"Ah . . . Kathleen, good morning," he said quickly.

"What are you looking for, Uncle Templeton?"

"Uh . . . nothing, Kathleen . . . I mean, I was just looking for, uh . . . for some coffee."

"Remember, we're out of coffee. But here is the tea," she said, walking toward the pantry.

"Ah, good—thank you," he said. "Good girl . . . thank you, Kathleen."

Two mornings later, Templeton Daniels was gone without a word of farewell.

That same day Katie's mother discovered that the cigar box, where she kept her household cash behind the sugar bin, was emptied of the thirty-five dollars she had been carefully hoarding.

She muttered something unladylike and left the pantry, vowing that the next time Templeton dared show his face around Rosewood, she would smack him across the mouth with her fist before she would think of inviting him into her house.

DESERTION

8

W ITH MONEY RUNNING OUT YET AGAIN, MRS. Clairborne and several of the Negro men loaded up the last of the previous year's cotton crop. It had been stored in the barn through the winter to sell later. The following morning, she and Katie were up early hitching two horses to the wagon to take it into Greens Crossing.

The war was nearly over. The South was in shambles. Confusion and turmoil were everywhere. Reports were coming in weekly that the Confederate army was in disarray and that men were leaving the front lines in droves. Mrs. Clairborne hoped her husband and two sons would be home soon. If they arrived without notice, she wanted to make sure there was at least a little cash on hand. She still hadn't decided how to tell them about the debts that were piling up. She knew Richard would be upset, but he would find out sooner or later.

She had sent Beulah down to the slave quarters with instructions to bring Mathias and Jeremiah up to the house to talk to her before she left. But just as Katie climbed up onto the wagon the big black woman came hurrying back as fast as her girth would allow.

"Miz Clairborne, ma'am, you gots ter come quick," she puffed. "Dere's trouble a brewin' down dere. You gotta come settle things."

"What it is, Beulah?" asked Katie's mother.

"Mathias en Jeb en some ob de others, dey's fixin' ter leave," said Beulah between gasps for breath.

"Leave!" exclaimed Mrs. Clairborne. "Leave where?"

"Dey said dey's free men. Da war's about ober an' slaves hab been set free. Dat's what dey're sayin,' Miz Clairborne. Dey said dey's slaves no mo' en dat dey's leabin'."

Mrs. Clairborne threw the reins around a rail and turned to follow on Beulah's heels.

She had only covered five or ten yards when she paused. How could she go into town with things as they were? Tomorrow would be no better. Nor the day after that. If the slaves were talking about deserting Rosewood, she had to be here every minute. She could not let this happen just when she was expecting Richard to return home.

She thought a moment more, then turned around. She glanced up at Katie waiting on the board seat of the wagon.

"Katie," she said, her mind racing ahead as she

spoke, "we can't wait with this load. But if I leave now, there's no telling what will happen here. I have to talk to Mathias and Jeb and the others. So I want you to take the wagon into town."

"By myself?" said Katie with uncertainty.

"You can do it," replied her mother. "You've gone with me dozens of times. You know the way well enough, and so do the horses."

"I can't, Mama."

"Yes you can—you have to. Just hold on to the reins, point the horses in the right direction, say *Gid'up* and give the reins a slap to go, and *Whoa* and pull gently back when you want to stop. The horses will do the rest. You've driven the team back and forth to the fields. This is just a little longer, that's all."

Katie's expression remained apprehensive.

"Take the wagon to Mr. Watson's loading dock by the train station," her mother went on. "He'll do the rest. When he's done, go to Henry at the livery and ask him to give the horses feed and water and help you get started back home."

As she spoke, Mrs. Clairborne untied the reins, climbed up onto the wagon beside Katie, and put the leather straps in her hands.

"You're fourteen now, Kathleen. That's one thing your uncle Templeton said that was indeed true—you're nearly a woman. After Mr. Watson gives you the money for the load, and while Henry's taking care of the horses, you go to the bank and see Mr. Taylor. You know who he is, don't you?"

"Yes, ma'am," Katie nodded slowly.

"Give him the money and tell him to put it into our account. Then go see Mrs. Hammond at the general store. Tell her we need ten pounds of salt, fifty pounds of sugar, twenty pounds of coffee beans, and two slabs of bacon. And pick up our mail while you're there. I'll write it down for you."

She climbed down and ran into the house while Beulah and Katie waited in silence. She returned a minute later and handed Katie the hastily scribbled note.

"Tell Mrs. Hammond to put these things on our account," she instructed, "then stop by the store again on your way back from Henry's and her man will load everything into the wagon. Once you've got it all, come straight back home."

"But, Mama . . ."

"You can do it, Kathleen—you have to." Her tone was firm.

Mrs. Clairborne slapped one of the horses on the rump. Then Katie's mother hurried away after Beulah toward the slave quarters. The wagon jostled off with a bewildered and apprehensive Katie at the reins.

Katie arrived in Greens Crossing two hours later. The horses plodded along in the direction of the train station, and a few minutes later Mr. Watson took charge.

"Your mama must be real proud of you, Miss Kathleen," he said, "bringing in this load all by yourself."

"Yes, sir," she replied as she watched his men unload the cotton.

"Before you know it, you'll be running a plantation of your own."

Katie didn't answer, but she was sure that wouldn't be anytime soon—if ever.

When the load had been transferred to the shed, he went inside for a minute, then returned with an envelope, which he handed up to Katie.

"Here you are, Miss Kathleen," said Watson. "Do you know what to do with it?"

"Yes, sir. I'm to take the horses to Henry, then take this money to Mr. Taylor."

"That's just fine, then." He smiled at her.

"Thank you, Mr. Watson," said Katie. "Would you please tell the horses to go," she asked timidly. "I don't know if they'll listen to me."

"Of course, Miss Kathleen." He laughed. "Gid'up!" he cried, giving one of the horses a slap.

They started slowly along the street, and Katie carefully pulled on the reins to get them to the livery stable.

"Why, hello, Miz Kathleen," said the black man as she approached. "Where's yo mama?"

"She had to stay home, Henry," replied Katie. "But she told me to have you take care of the horses while I go to the bank and the store."

"You kin count on me, Miz Kathleen," he said with a smile. "Here, lemme hep you down."

He took her hand, stood her up on the footboard, then guided her to the ground.

"Any mo word from yo papa?" he asked.

"No, sir."

"Well, dey say da war's like ter be ober by'n by, so 'twon't be long 'for he'll be comin', I'm thinkin'."

"Yes, sir. I have to go see Mr. Taylor and Mrs. Hammond now. Then I'll come back for the wagon."

"Well, you's sho' growin' up mighty fast, Miz Kathleen."

At the general store, Mrs. Hammond's eagle eye had already seen Katie ride into town alone. She was one who took quite a different view of Katie's capabilities than would either black Henry or white Mr. Watson. A natural curiosity, along with a persistent scowl, were both in evidence as Katie opened her door a few minutes later, sending the little bell tinkling into motion above it.

The proprietress wasted no time on superficialities.

"Where's your mama, Kathleen?" she demanded.

"At home, ma'am. She wanted me to pick up some things."

"All by yourself?"

"Yes, ma'am. Here's the list. And the mail, please."

"Well . . . I declare . . ." muttered Mrs. Hammond, taking the list and glancing through it. She prided herself on knowing everything about everybody in this community. And anything out of the ordinary she took as a personal affront.

When Katie rode back into Rosewood six hours after her departure, exhausted and famished, her mother ran out of the house to meet her. The supplies were in the back of the wagon, but one look at her daughter's face showed that she was about to faint from hunger and thirst.

"Oh, Katie dear," exclaimed Mrs. Clairborne, "I forgot to give you anything to eat. You poor thing!"

She helped Katie down, hurried her inside, washed her face, gave her a glass of water to drink, and sat her down at the kitchen table.

"Did you have any trouble?" she asked.

"No, Mama," replied Katie, already beginning to revive. "Except that I got tired."

"What did I tell you—I knew you would be fine. I'm proud of you, Kathleen."

"What about the darkies, Mama?"

Mrs. Clairborne shook her head.

"Mathias and Jeb left, along with their wives," she said. "But I convinced the others to stay."

"Where will they go?" asked Katie.

"I don't know," sighed her mother. "They said they have kin up North. I gave them each two dollars, which is about all the money I had left. I don't know what they'll do. Colored folks traveling alone like that . . . I pray no harm comes to them. There's said to be roving bands of deserters and ex-soldiers and marauders everywhere. I don't like to think what might happen to them. . . ."

"Will bad men like that hurt Papa and Joseph and Caleb?"

"I hope not, Kathleen. We must remember to pray for them."

"When will Papa come home, Mama?"

"Soon, I hope, dear : . . very soon."

"What will he say about Mathias and Jeb?"

"He will be angry, I'm sure."

As they talked, Katie downed several slices of bread and swallowed two glasses of milk, and suddenly drowsiness began to overtake her.

Her mother took her hand and led her upstairs to her room, and within minutes she was tucked in bed and sound asleep.

BONE WEARY, Rosalind Clairborne sat at the kitchen table of Rosewood that same night, head resting on her hands. It was late. A single kerosene lamp burned from across the table, illuminating a sheet of paper in front of her.

For thirty minutes she had been staring at it, trying to turn the jumble of figures into some sense that her tired brain could understand. But she couldn't concentrate long enough. Mr. Taylor's words from their last encounter kept coming back to haunt her.

"It's out of my control now, Rosalind," he had said. "I simply can't in good conscience carry your debt much longer."

She had been trying to stretch the pitifully small amount of money left in the Clairborne account as far as she could. But now she had missed the last two payments on their loan, and the bank manager had spoken to her about it.

"It isn't fair to others in the community," Mr. Taylor had continued. "Surely you understand. It puts the bank, and everyone, at risk."

"But what am I supposed to do?" Mrs. Clairborne replied, trying to squeeze back the tears and keep her voice from trembling. "We needed supplies. I can't let

Katie and the darkies go without food."

She went on to explain as best she could that there wasn't much besides cotton growing at Rosewood this year—she just hadn't gotten around to getting in the food crops, and the garden was dwindling.

"Surely you've got potatoes, and the wheat."

"Yes, I don't suppose we're actually going to starve, but you remember the hailstorm—that didn't help either. It has just been a very hard year, and . . ."

She turned away. She *couldn't* let Mr. Taylor see her cry!

"I understand," he said, a slight note of sympathy creeping into his tone. "I will continue to do what I can. But you simply must begin making some regular payments. You cannot continue putting all the money into your account and then spending it without paying down the balance."

Still turned away, Mrs. Clairborne swallowed hard, nodded, then rose and left the bank. And now with his words still ringing in her ears, her eyes filled again with tears at the mortification she felt being beholden to everyone. She tried again to focus on the paper lying on the table.

But it was no use. She pushed it away with a sigh, then dabbed at her eyes.

Even as she did, a sound intruded into her thoughts. She lifted her head and turned toward the back of the house. It was much too late in the evening for visitors . . . but she could have sworn she heard horses!

All thoughts of hailstorms, money, and past-due loans instantly vanished as she scrambled to her feet.

Heart pounding, the next instant she was hurrying into the parlor. She unlocked the gun case with trembling fingers and lifted out one of the rifles.

Within seconds she was back in the kitchen, turned down the flame on the lamp, then moved across the floor in the darkness to the window. Kneeling down and pulling the curtain carefully to one side, she peered out into the night, which was lit only by a sliver of moon.

At first she could see nothing. Gradually her eyes were able to make out the vague forms of three figures on horseback. They appeared out of the gloom from the direction of Greens Crossing and were slowly approaching the house.

Heart beating so rapidly she could hear its pounding inside her head, she felt a lump rise in her throat. She raised the rifle and sighted down the long barrel.

A chill swept through her as she targeted the dark silhouette of the man riding in the middle . . . that slight slouch to the right in the saddle—it looked just like—

The rifle slipped from her hands and crashed on the floor. Then she was on her feet and out the door, running down the steps toward them.

"Richard!" she cried, tears flowing down her face. "Richard . . . is it really you?"

The rider was off his horse now too, but had time only to take a step or two before the arms of his wife smothered into silence whatever words he might have been going to utter. The next several seconds were consumed by the sound of her relieved sobs, while he returned her embrace, stroking her hair and murmuring her name quietly into her ear.

"Oh, Richard . . . I thought you would never come home! I can hardly believe you're actually here . . . am I not dreaming this?"

"It is really us, Rosalind. Believe me, we're happier to be here than you could possibly be to see us. It feels like we've been gone ten years."

Rosalind gradually came to herself and glanced up at the other two riders.

"Oh, Joseph . . . Caleb!" Her arms stretched toward them. "How exhausted you must be! Come into the house and I'll make you something to eat."

"A bed, Mother—that's all we need," murmured Caleb as he dropped wearily out of his saddle and into his mother's embrace.

"Speak for yourself," chided his brother. "I've been dreaming of Mother's stew for three years!"

"You take the boys inside, Rosalind," said Richard Clairborne. "I'll unsaddle the horses and be right there. And I'm with Joseph—some stew would go down right pleasant."

Rosalind Clairborne took her two sons' arms and led them inside, bursting with more joy in her heart than she imagined she would ever be capable of feeling again.

9

K ATIE STRUGGLED OUT OF A DEEP SLEEP. SHE LAY for a moment in her bed, wondering about the sounds that had awakened her. Gradually she drifted back toward slumber. But a few moments later she was wide awake, scrambling out from under her blankets. She heard muffled voices drifting up the stairway.

Her bare feet made no sound as she hurried out of her bedroom and tiptoed down the stairs in her nightgown. Heart pounding, she paused in the kitchen doorway, taking in a scene she had imagined in her mind for months, but never thought she would actually see again.

There stood her father and mother, arms intertwined, standing in the middle of the room talking earnestly in low tones. Behind them, Joseph and Caleb sat at the table, devouring the remains of the corn bread and bean stew from supper.

Katie stood silently for several seconds. She could see the lines of fatigue in her father's face and his long hair, now amply streaked with gray, curling around his ears. His eyes looked tired and careworn even as he gazed tenderly into his wife's face. Soon they all became aware of another presence in the room.

"Katie!" exclaimed Richard Clairborne, releasing his wife and covering the distance across the floor in three giant strides. He scooped her into his arms, nearly lifting her off the floor.

"Hello, Papa," said Katie shyly, almost as if she were being embraced by a stranger.

"I can't tell you how I missed you, Katie," her father said, his cheek against her hair. He pushed back a little to look at her. "And you've grown! You must be eight inches taller than the last time I saw you. But I'd know you anywhere."

Her face buried in his coat, with its smells of travel, dust, and gunpowder, Katie thought she had never felt so contented in all her life. Not even the smell of a man who hadn't bathed in a long time could take away her happiness.

As her father released her and she stepped back, she saw dark red splotches on the sleeve of his coat.

"Papa, what's that?" she asked, then drew back as realization struck her.

"Never you mind what it is, Katie," he answered. "All that's behind us now . . . behind us forever. It's all over and we're home—that's all you need to know."

"You got more of this corn bread?" came a voice from the table. "It's uncommonly good, Mother."

As Rosalind bustled about setting every scrap of food she could find on the table, Katie now moved slowly toward the two ravenous young men, whom she could only half remember as once being boys she had played with.

"Hey, little girl!" said Caleb, reaching out a hand

and tussling her hair. "Papa's right, you done grown up. Ain't that right, Joseph?"

"She's turned into a lady, all right, haven't you, Katie?"

"I suppose so, sir."

"*Sir?* What're you talking about, Katie! I ain't no sir, I'm your big brother Joe!"

"Don't pay any attention to them, Katie," laughed Katie's mother. "They just grew to become men and forgot their manners."

"That's what war does to a body, Rosalind," said Katie's father, shaking his head. "It's a horrible thing, and I hope nobody in this country has to go to war like that again."

The kitchen fell silent as their thoughts unconsciously turned to the son and brother the war had forever taken from them. Even the memory of that tragic loss, however, could not dampen the enthusiasm of the reunion. Soon mother and father and the two sons were laughing and talking and eating, while Katie sat silently and contentedly at her mother's side, drinking it all in.

"We've got bad money problems, Richard," Mrs. Clairborne eventually said, and the atmosphere took on a more somber tone. "Most of the darkies are gone . . . I had to take out a loan at the bank."

Richard reached for her hand. "I can't believe—"

"I had no choice. I didn't know what else to do." Rosalind's eyes fell to her lap.

"Well, no matter," said Clairborne. "We'll get all that straightened around. Me and the boys are back, and we'll get Rosewood back to normal."

The next several days were blissful for both Katie and Rosalind Clairborne. No longer did Rosewood's fate rest solely in their hands. The men were back—to make decisions and do the hard work, and mostly just to know what to do.

The first day Mr. and Mrs. Clairborne walked all about Rosewood as Katie's mother explained what she had tried to do, what she hadn't been able to do, showing her husband the nearly empty slave quarters, the broken fences, and the partially planted fields.

The frustration at having been gone for so long was clearly evident on Richard Clairborne's face as he saw to what a state the once proud plantation had fallen. But he was not one to mope about, and that same afternoon, he and Joseph and Caleb busily set to repairing a stretch of fence near the woods.

TWO DAYS LATER Katie sat at the kitchen table watching her mother knead a batch of bread. She was supposed to be peeling potatoes for their supper, but her hands were still, though her thoughts were not. "Mama," she finally began, "why don't Caleb and Joseph want to talk about the war? When I ask them questions, they just pat my head and change the subject."

Rosalind's hands stopped too and she stared out the window. "I know, Katie—I've noticed that also. I think it will take time for all of us to get over the long separation and the awful memories to become a family again." She turned back to Katie with a smile and buried her hands again in the dough.

At the stove across the kitchen, Beulah was just pulling a sweet potato pie from the oven. "Hmm, hmm," she exclaimed. "My boys are going to have themselves a supper jes' like da ol' times," she added. "Good, warm food, a roof ober dere heads, hard work every day—dere souls will be back wiff dere bodies in no time."

Katie and Rosalind smiled at each other.

"Thank you, Beulah," said Rosalind. "You've been a faithful part of our family all these years."

"Yes'm" was Beulah's only reply.

TRAGEDY

10

EVERY DAY ROSEWOOD RETURNED MORE AND MORE to normal. Beulah's deep contralto could occasionally be heard singing from the kitchen. With a newly slaughtered pig and calf, and a batch of potatoes dug up, there was more food for her to prepare than there had been in months. Smoke rose over the smokehouse, where most of the meat hung, and a fresh barrel of brine was prepared in the cellar for the rest. Flour and cornmeal were once again in plentiful supply after a morning's session at the mill. And except for the problems at the bank, Rosalind began to think they had survived this after all.

Her husband had been too busy, however, to get into town. He kept saying he would get to it in a few days, just as soon as he and the boys got the most important things attended to at Rosewood. But Rosalind could tell he was no more anxious to go hat in hand to Mr. Taylor than she had been.

Exactly eight days after her father's return, once again Katie was suddenly awakened in the middle of the night from a sound sleep. Startled, she sat straight up in her bed.

As she came to herself, she recognized the ominous thunder of riders approaching. From the bedroom across the landing, she heard her father shouting to wake Joseph and Caleb as he sprinted downstairs and to the gun cabinet. Several gunshots cracked through the night from the direction of the slave quarters.

Groggy and bewildered, Katie's brain tried to make sense of the confusion.

Horrifying sounds were everywhere. Outside, shouts and yells, pounding hooves and frightened whinnies from what seemed a dozen or more horses screamed through the night.

In the house she heard more yelling . . . then footsteps hurrying up the stairs, and the door burst open.

"Katie . . . Katie, get up!" said a voice in a terrified whisper.

Katie could see nothing as her mother shook her fully awake.

"Get up, Kathleen . . . get up and come quickly!"

In a sleepy daze Katie swung her feet over the side of the bed. Mrs. Clairborne pulled her to her feet and

Katie struggled to stand.

Suddenly gunfire exploded outside, and her mother let out an involuntary scream. Terrible shouts echoed everywhere. Katie was too frightened to wonder what this confused nightmare could mean.

Tugging her along by the hand, Mrs. Clairborne hurried her daughter downstairs and into the parlor. She stopped, threw back the rug, yanked up the trapdoor, and pushed Katie down the cellar ladder, then followed herself. Katie sat down on the cold floor, trembling from cold and shock.

"I'll be back in a few minutes, Katie," said her mother frantically, throwing an old quilt around her shoulders. "I've got to go back up and get a few things. Don't make a peep. Do you hear me—not a sound!"

Mrs. Clairborne turned and hurried up the rickety ladder. A moment later Katie heard the wood door clunk back down onto the floorboards. She was absolutely alone, still wearing her nightclothes, sitting in pitch-black darkness beneath the floor of the house.

Above and outside, the terrifying sounds continued, though she could not make out what they were through the floor and rug and furniture.

Somewhere a door banged open, heavily booted feet tramped above her—suddenly a terrible crash made her jump where she sat. Katie didn't know it, but her mother's glass china cabinet had just fallen over, sending plates and dishes and cups spewing in broken pieces across the floor.

Shouts followed. More doors slamming. Another crash, and sharp blasts of gunfire. Voices she didn't know—screaming . . . what she thought was her mother's voice. More screams, more explosions that seemed to go on for hours. Running footsteps, a few shouts . . . then gradually the muffled sound of horses retreating in the distance.

And then finally . . . silence.

What she had been listening to was foreboding and terrible. Even with the quilt around her, Katie's body began to shake with undefined terror.

Afraid to move, afraid to breathe, afraid to think, Katie sat in a black stupor. How long she remained huddled in the dark corner where her mother had tucked her, she had no idea.

Why doesn't Mama come back? was all she could think.

But she heard nothing. The great Clairborne house was quiet as a graveyard.

Eventually—how long was it, an hour . . . maybe two—Katie fell into a restless sleep.

When she came to herself she was slumped on the dirt floor, clutching the quilt around her, so cold her arms and legs and feet were numb. All she could think was that she had had a terrible nightmare, was still in the middle of it, and would wake up before long in her own bed. But finally sleep overtook her again.

Morning came. But Katie didn't know it. Not the tiniest crack of light entered the cellar. All remained silent above.

Katie gradually began to feel things that told her she wasn't dreaming and she wasn't in her bed—like the growling in her stomach and the freezing cold in every inch of her body.

Finally she sat up, moved her stiff arms and legs, and pulled herself to her feet. She felt her way to the ladder. Slowly she put one foot ahead of the other and began climbing. Her head bumped against the cellar door. She pushed against it, but it wouldn't budge.

With all the strength she could muster, Katie struggled to raise the trapdoor. Finally a chink of light came through a tiny crack as she strained to hold the door up. Now she knew it was daytime for sure.

Whimpering with cold and fear, she gave one last shove with all her might. Something rolled off the door with a dull thud, and it swung up and back on creaking hinges.

"Mama—Mama!" cried Katie. "Mama, where are you!"

Nothing but silence answered the dying echo of her voice. Katie took another step up and pushed herself the rest of the way into the room.

Katie's hand went to her mouth. Destruction was everywhere. Windows were broken. The furniture was turned over. Pictures and vases and plates and glassware had been shattered and strewn about. The china cabinet wasn't the only case on the floor. Several bookshelves had suffered the same fate. Books and pieces of china were scattered all through the parlor. Her mother's piano was still upright, but had a big gash on top where something had crashed on it. Her own violin beside it was shattered into three pieces, held together only by the now useless strings. Seeing the sight broke through Katie's shock. Music and books were as much a part of her life as her special place in the woods. She began to cry and tears poured down her face.

Katie tried to call her mother again. But her trembling lips could hardly form the word.

Hers was not an imagination capable of even dreaming such horror. But the sights before her were enough to fill her with mute shock.

What confronted her delicate young innocence was a hurricane of death and destruction.

She stumbled across the room in a trance. Before she could find her voice again, the sight of her mother's body lying across the doorway into the kitchen, her dress torn and bloodstained, made calling out again useless.

Katie's knees began to buckle. She gagged once or twice and an icy chill seized heart and brain together, more despairing than any cold she had ever felt.

Shaking and crying, she gagged again and looked away, then made herself turn back into the parlor. Now she saw the bloodied body of one of her brothers slumped beneath the window, the rifle still clutched in his stiff hands, and that of her father next to the trapdoor, where his body had slid off it as Katie had climbed out of the cellar.

Katie stood, incapable of movement, unable to utter a sound, unconscious that she was now an orphan . . . unconscious of anything. She only stood rigidly with arms clutching herself, all physical and mental functions frozen into uselessness. She was unaware that even her few movements across the floor had already stained her feet and nightgown with the blood of her proud Southern heritage.

How long she stood in a stupor of shock, she wouldn't have been able to say. Death was all around. Blood was splattered everywhere—some dried black, some in pools so thick it was still red.

Suddenly Katie heard footsteps behind her. In the midst of the awful silence, the sound frightened her back to reality.

She nearly leapt out of her skin and spun around. Her muscles tensed in readiness to flee.

There stood a lanky black girl near her own age whom she had never seen before.

That girl was me.

MAYME

11

NOW I RECKON IT'S TIME YOU HEAR A LITTLE ABOUT my part of this story.

I know how it is when you're trying to keep track of what's going on, and the storyteller jumps about till you get so confused you can't tell what happened when. And now here I am doing that same thing.

But sometimes it just seems that's the best way to tell something. And like I said, I'm so used to having Katie beside me telling her part of this that I'm a little befuddled myself knowing how to explain it. So I reckon you'll just have to keep track of it the best you can—which I'm sure you'll be able to do—until I somehow get the whole thing laid out for you.

I may have said earlier that Katie's brain was in the habit of moving a mite slow, though her imagination was alive as could be. I was just the opposite. She hadn't had to think or make decisions. But I had. Where she was a dreamer, I was practical. There isn't a thing wrong with either kind of person. I reckon it takes both to make a world, and if we were all alike it'd be a pretty boring place.

I *had* to be practical. I'm not saying I didn't have time to dream, because you can dream and let your imagination go where it wants whatever else you might be doing. But the work was hard, and I didn't really think much about dreaming. I just did what I had to do. That included telling stories, like I said, but somehow that was different, more like just a way to pass the time.

I was the oldest of five kids. I grew up telling stories to little Samuel, and after him came three more little ones, Rachel, Robert, and Thelma. Seems my mama was always expecting a baby, and I had to not just tell the young'uns stories, but I had to take care of them too—feed them and change their dirty diapers and wash their clothes and anything else that was needed while Mama was out working the master's garden or trying to get our clothes clean down at the stream.

So I learned mighty quick to fend for myself and

do what needed to be done.

It was a hard life, being a girl in a slave family. Mama depended on me, and that's how life was. My daddy and all the men worked in the master's fields all day. When he and the men came back to the slave quarters every night, they were so tuckered out, it was all they could do to sit at the table and eat the watery stew Mama and the other women had made that day.

It was a hard life for women too, and for children like me. Everybody had to work—work was what we did. It was the only life we knew. When the sun came up, we got out of bed and started working. We worked till we fell asleep that night.

But Sundays were different. After the chores were done, the master let us have the whole afternoon and evening to ourselves. That's when the old men told stories and people gathered round. Then in the evening there would be a big fire and lots of singing.

How I loved the singing! It wasn't the kind of music Katie and her mother made from notes on a page that somebody had written down. Our music came from our insides—from our souls, I reckon you'd say, and from our feelings. Our music was about us and about our way of life, and sometimes it could lift a body right up to heaven, it was so pretty.

That's where I started to learn about religion too, from the singing and the stories. It seems that the harder the times got, the more we sang songs about people in the Bible, about others who'd had to work hard, who'd suffered too.

But Monday always came again, and then the work would begin the minute we got up.

But children don't know a hard life from an easy one. Youngsters just cope with what they've got to cope with and don't think about it.

I didn't think about it either. I just did what I had to do. I reckon that's where I got my common sense and practicality, in the same way that Katie hadn't yet learned to do too much for herself. Maybe that's why God saw fit to bring me and Katie together—so that our differences could fit together to help us be more than either of us could have been by ourselves.

The man I called "Papa" died when I was twelve. I don't know why. I think he got sick from something. Death was part of slave life. Somebody was always dying. Mama was expecting again. The master said she could stay on in the cabin till the new baby was two. Then she'd need to marry again or be sold off.

Mama cried for a day or two. Then the tears dried up, and we went on doing what we had always done.

Sometime after that I came upon Mama one day sitting alone on the bed with a strange kind of look on her face, kinda happy and sad at the same time. I guess it's what you'd call nostalgic, but I didn't know that word then. She was holding a funny-shaped little blue thing.

"What's that?" I asked.

"Just a reminder of a long-ago time, chil'," she said, smiling that peculiar smile again.

"What does that word on it mean?"

"Dat ain't a word, chil'. It's a reminder of the tears

of life dat sometimes a body can't help, an' some memories are best left unremembered."

"Where'd you get it, Mama?" I asked.

She looked at me deep in the eyes, then down at the pin, then up at me again and smiled. Then she put it away with her Bible, and I don't recollect seeing it again, excepting every once in a while on a special day like Christmas when she'd hang it from a chain around her neck. But she never answered my question . . . and I never asked about it again.

Nothing much changed right after that. My grandpapa lived with us too after Grandmama died, but he was getting too old to work in the fields. The master wasn't too happy about our cabin full of people with none of us working in the fields. When the new baby was two months old, Mama went to work out in the fields with the men.

A while after I got to be fifteen, I recall a day when the master and two of his sons came down to the quarter. He visited a few minutes with Grandpapa. Then Grandpapa called out to fetch me and Samuel, who was now eleven. We came and stood while the master looked us over head to toe. Behind him, the master's oldest son was looking at me real ugly-like.

We both knew what it was all about. Slaves had value to their masters in one of three ways. Strong men worked. Strong women had babies. And children were raised to do one or the other—or else be sold. Boys grew up to give the master more work. Girls grew up to give him more babies. If he didn't think they'd do either very well, or if he needed what money he thought they'd bring, he'd sell them. The time had come when the master was thinking what would be best to do with me and Samuel when our time came.

He looked Samuel over, probably asking himself when he could start taking Papa's place in the fields. He was feeling the muscles of Sam's arms and looking over his shoulders and chest, wondering how much he was going to fill out, while my brother stood there staring straight ahead still as a statue. Then he came over to me to do the same. People nowadays probably think it a pretty awful thing for a man to do, but back in those days a slave was his master's property and he did whatever he pleased with them, same as he would a wagon or a cow or a saddle.

He walked up to me and started looking me over too. He stuck a couple fingers in my mouth and pried it open so he could see all my teeth. Why didn't I try to bite his fingers off, you're maybe wondering. Because I didn't want my back bleeding from a whipping, that's why. I'd already had two whippings in my life, the worst from the master's son, and I didn't want to ever get another one.

Then he stood back and looked at my front, and his eyes paused a few seconds at my breasts, which were starting to bulge out a bit under my dirty apron. Out of the corner of my eye I saw his two sons wink at each other, and I didn't much like the way they were looking at me. Then the master nodded to himself and turned back to my grandfather.

"A mite scrawny," he said, "and not much of a looker. Still, she might fetch seventy-five dollars. You got any of your young bucks in mind to bed her down? Otherwise I'll get what I can for her."

I didn't hear what my grandfather said.

It didn't matter. I didn't get bedded by any of the sixteen- or seventeen-year-old slave boys, or sold either.

Because two weeks later is when the renegade soldiers came.

MASSACRE

12

I DIDN'T KNOW AT THE TIME WHO THE SOLDIERS WERE. I didn't know that the war was all but over, or that the South was breaking up and in chaos, or that deserters or marauders were roaming everywhere. All I knew was that a war had been going on between North and South, that the two sides wore blue and gray, and that somehow we slaves were in the middle of it. Sometimes we'd see soldiers riding by, and once or twice you could hear cannon fire way off in the distance. But mostly we went about our work.

Some said the soldiers from the North, Mr. Lincoln's soldiers, were trying to set us free. But it was hard to think of any white man—even if they wore blue and talked funny—as friends to colored folks.

I was down at the creek fetching water when I heard

horses galloping toward the shacks and barns of our colored town—which now I reckon folks would call a collection of hovels—where we slaves lived. Our men were mostly in the fields, so no one could have put up much of a fight. It was all over too quick for that.

A thunder of riders was coming so fast I could feel the ground shaking under me. With the shouts and horses and the dust and dirt flying, it looked to my eyes like a hundred men bearing straight for the houses, yelling and shooting. I heard screams from Mama and the rest of the women. Then gunfire and more shouts. Terrible sounds filled the air all around me. Horrible screams and loud explosions from the guns all mingled together in an uproar that was deafening.

I dropped my water bucket and ran toward the quarter. But about halfway back I stopped and hid behind a tree. Whatever was going on, it was clear it wouldn't do a girl like me a bit of good to run out into the middle of it.

What I saw from behind the tree filled me with more terror than I'd ever felt before or since. If I hadn't been wide awake, and known I was awake, I'd have figured it for a nightmare. It was as grisly as the worst nightmare you could imagine.

The riders were shooting and trampling everybody and knocking everything over and riding around recklessly with their horses kicking and rearing all over the place. They were shouting out horrible curses, and when I think back on it now, I figure they were taking out their anger toward the North and Mr. Lincoln on this little group of slaves, like we were the ones who had caused it all. The horsemen—and I later found out there were fourteen of them—were laughing and cussing like they were enjoying it.

What kind of men would do that? I've been asking myself that all my life. What kind of people actually enjoy hurting others? I can't think of anything to call them but savage as a meat ax, just plumb evil. If ever there's a day of reckoning when all the things everybody's done gets put right by God, then bad men like that will surely face some horrible punishment for such awful deeds. Seeing what I saw that day sure made me a believer in hell, because no hell could be too bad for men who could do what they did.

At the time I was too stunned by what I was seeing to hate. But hatred would rise up in my heart soon enough. And it was a hatred I didn't feel guilty for either. They were the kind of men who did evil that oughta be hated.

They wore shabby, dirty gray uniforms and looked scraggly and mean. Children were screaming and running every which way, and chickens and pigs in their pens were cackling and squawking. Dust was flying about, and I reckon blood was already mixed with it all over the ground. But from where I was, I couldn't see that yet.

Then my grandpapa came running out of the house with the master's shotgun that was kept there in case of trouble. I saw the fire explode out of the end of the barrel, and the sound ricocheted through all the commotion. One of the riders tumbled off his horse with the side of his face blown off. The next instant a dozen shots followed, and my poor grandpapa was jerked to the side with the bullets and then fell with half a dozen of them through his heart and head. I was terrified and I could not have moved if my life depended on it.

One of the riders spun his horse around, waving his pistol in the air, trampling over Grandpapa's body with the horse's hooves, then turned and shot the body two or three more times where it lay. It seemed to incite the rest of them all the more. They went wild with rage. The man waving the pistol let out a great laugh, then tore off in a huge circle around the place, shooting in a frenzy.

Then I realized he was riding straight toward me!

I was paralyzed. I couldn't even breathe.

It was just an instant, but as he came riding in my direction, yelling wildly and with that evil fire in his eye, I looked into that face and knew I'd never forget it as long as I lived.

He hadn't shaved in a while. His whiskers were kind of reddish, though a dirty gray army hat covered up the hair on his head. He had a thick moustache, though not the kind that spin out into a point like some white men's. But the eyes are what I remember most. I wasn't close enough to see what color they were. But they were wide, so that the white went all around the inside part, and seemed to be flashing with fire itself. The only way I know to describe them is to say they were wicked eyes.

The next moment my wits came back to me. What

was I doing staring at him! Did I want him to shoot me in the head too!

Fearing I was about to be a goner, I shrunk behind the tree trunk, sucking in my tummy as skinny as I could make it, terrified he was going to see me. I heard a few more gunshots. One of them hit my tree, and a piece of bark splintered off and flew back past my ear.

I figured he'd seen me and that I would be dead in less than a minute. I don't mind admitting that I was shaking from head to foot and clinging to the back side of that tree with my eyes squeezed shut like I was a baby at her mama's breast.

But then he spun his horse around and went galloping back toward the others, still shooting wildly and yelling like he was corned with a brick in his hat or was crazy. Maybe both.

Then all of a sudden as quickly as it had begun, they rode off, dust flying up behind them, their yelling voices receding in the distance.

And maybe half a minute later came the quiet. The worst quiet I'd ever heard in my life.

Just like I'll never forget that man's face, I'll never forget that silence after they rode off. I reckon somewhere in the back of my head I must have still heard them for a spell longer, because they had ridden out toward the fields where the men had been working. There was more gunfire in the distance when they reached our men. But that was over in another minute or two.

Then came an even deeper stillness than before.

The chickens were still squawking, and now and then I heard the grunt of a pig.

But there were no people sounds. No mother crying. No baby whimpering. Nothing.

It was a deathly, eerie, terrible quiet.

For a long time I just kept standing there, trembling behind the tree. I knew the riders were gone. But I was afraid to come out. I was afraid to look. I don't know how long I stood there. When I finally came out, there were no sounds anywhere—not even off in the distance . . . not from the fields . . . not from the plantation . . . not anywhere.

And I knew why.

AWAY

13

BY THE TIME I CREPT OUT FROM BEHIND THE TREE, afternoon was already getting on. Somehow I suppose I knew the riders wouldn't be back. Why would they come back? There wasn't anything else they could possibly do.

Who can describe what a person feels at a dreadful time like that? I can't say I was *afraid*. I was stunned, horrified at what I saw around me. I figured our own men must be dead too since none of them came back and I heard nothing from the direction of the fields.

But I didn't know for sure. And whether Josepha and the other house slaves were still alive and the master and his family, I didn't even think about at first. Mostly I just knew I had to pull foot in a hurry and skedaddle out of there.

Of course now the history books call these few days the massacre of Shenandoah County, and everybody knows about the gang of outlaw Confederate deserters called Bilsby's Marauders. But from where I stood behind that tree, and where I stood after I stumbled up toward what had been my home, all I knew was that I had just heard and seen my mama and my brothers and sisters and my grandfather murdered with my own ears and eyes, and that this place would never be my home again.

I buried them all—Mama and Grandpapa and Samuel and the three younger ones. They were the only family I had, and it was the last thing I could do for them. I couldn't take the time, and I didn't have the heart or strength for it either, to try to bury the other women and children. I just couldn't. There were too many. I did my best to avoid the body of the soldier Grandpapa'd shot. Blood was all over him, and I didn't want to look at what was left of his face.

I didn't worry about getting them too deep in the ground, just enough to feel that I'd done what was right and to keep the flies and birds away. Even before I was done, I'd made up my mind I had to leave. I didn't know where I'd go, but I couldn't stay there.

People always ask me if I cried, or if I was afraid.

People are so curious to know what I felt.

No, I didn't cry. Not yet at least. I was too numb. I don't know what I felt inside. Like I said, I was too shocked to feel something I can describe in words. I found the shovel and dug the holes and pushed what was left of my family into them . . . I reckon I did it by instinct. I didn't think about it. I just found myself with the shovel in my hand starting to whack at the ground. I'd seen enough black folks buried that it was just something I knew you were supposed to do. It took me the rest of the day and into the evening.

But by and by I began to realize what kind of serious trouble I likely was in. I knew enough about the war and the state of slaves in the South to realize that a fifteen-year-old black girl, alone, was going to be in a considerable fix if she ran into someone who maybe wasn't too inclined to be friendly toward her. Worse—if she ran into the kind of men who had just murdered her family. I probably should have gone up to the big house to see if Josepha and the master's family were alive. But I wasn't thinking none too clearly.

If your skin happened to be black in those days, by the time you were old enough to know your own name, you knew that the other kind of people in the world, people with white skin, didn't think much of folks with curly black hair and colored skin—whether it was brown like mine or tan or dark black, it didn't make a spit of difference. And they didn't usually go out of their way to be nice to them unless you had a real good master. I had heard about slaves who had nice masters. And even if I did happen to run into Yankees from the North, though I'd never actually seen one of them Jonathans, as we Southerners called them, in my life, I didn't figure it'd make much difference. North or South, white folks didn't like colored folks much. That's just the way it was.

So I knew I'd be in a heap of trouble if I was found by *any* white man. I didn't know what might have happened at the plantation house, but I didn't like the idea of being found by the master either. He'd be needing more darkies to keep things going. He'd probably want to bed me down with somebody first chance he got—maybe one of his own sons, or even the master himself, since all our men were gone. And I didn't like the thought of that one bit.

So as soon as I was done with the burying, and said the Lord's Prayer, then I set off walking across the fields away from the plantation house.

I did one other thing before I left. I went over to the chicken pen and opened the gate, and the same with the pigs. I didn't know if black people would ever be free. But it seemed to me that those animals weren't going to be much good to anybody now, especially if they didn't get fed, so they at least might as well be free to find their own way.

Then I left.

Already dusk was closing in. I didn't know which direction I was going. I had nothing in mind except just to walk and stay out of sight. I don't figure anybody who'd been through what I had thinks about eating, and I didn't. I hadn't eaten in a long time. My stomach was in such knots it couldn't have kept food in it anyway. I drank from a few creeks as I went.

After a while it got real dark. I'd probably walked a long way because I was feeling mighty tired. It's a good thing too. The weariness eventually helped me sleep. I kept walking as the moon came up, and I kept walking and walking, probably for half the night. Then I came to a sheltered little wood that I liked the looks of. It wasn't too cold that night, so I just lay down in the middle of some bushes and went to sleep.

I woke up sometime after dawn. I could tell the sun hadn't been up too long. I was chilly and a little damp.

The first thing that came into my head was what a horrifying nightmare I'd had.

I stretched a bit, waking up enough to start wondering where I was.

Then the nightmare that wasn't a nightmare came crashing back into my soul with the reality that makes memories so different from dreams. Images of dead bodies suddenly filled my head. My stomach gagged and I was sick for several seconds. I wished I could have just kept sleeping forever, and never have woken up. It was the worst waking up I ever had in my born days.

But the only way to cope with the awful pain of the memory was to move. I couldn't think. It was too dreadful to think. I had to *do* something. So I got up and started walking again, still without an idea where I was going.

How long I walked, I don't know. I think I took another drink someplace, but I lost track of events and direction as well as time. I likely wandered around in circles some.

All of a sudden I realized I'd stumbled straight into the yard of a great big plantation house. I hadn't been paying attention to where I was going, and there weren't any sounds coming from anywhere. I just looked up and there the house was in front of me. It was a big, fancy two-story house, all white, with columns all the way around it and several big oaks growing in the front.

I stopped in my tracks. It wasn't my master's plantation, that much I knew. It was a lot bigger, and I didn't recognize anything.

I stood for a minute or two listening, wondering why it was so quiet. I started walking slowly toward the house, a tad scared, but starting to feel hungry enough that I wanted to find something to eat. I wandered around toward the back, where there were a few more buildings. As I got closer I began to realize that things didn't look right. A buggy was overturned, some of the fence was broken. And as I looked up at the house I saw some windows broken.

All of a sudden I almost stumbled over someone lying on the ground in front of me. I looked down at the body of a young white man who looked to be about twenty. One look at his face and I knew that he was cold as a wagon tire.

I don't know why I didn't turn around and take off running right then. But after what I'd seen yesterday,

I just stepped over him and continued on. A few yards farther I saw a black woman who'd been shot too and a black man nearby.

I walked toward the house.

It was way too quiet. From off somewhere around the other side, I heard two or three dogs barking. I don't know where they'd been, but now they were coming back, and I didn't feel like trying to explain myself to them.

The back door of the house was ajar. I gave it a little shove and it swung open.

I wasn't really getting my mind around things too good yet. Maybe I figured if everyone had been killed here too, that at least maybe there'd be something around I could eat. Why I had been leery of being found by my own master but was just going ahead and barging into some *other* white man's house, I don't know. Doesn't make much sense as I look back on it. But the place seemed so deserted, I probably figured nobody was around but dead folks, like the man in the yard. It seemed like the same evil men must have been here too and killed everyone. And I sure did need food before I keeled over.

The minute I stepped inside I saw that the whole place had been pillaged, just like what had happened where I lived. There was stuff broken all over the floor.

Slowly I walked into what I took to be the kitchen. I saw another body on the floor, this time a white woman, older than the young fellow outside, maybe forty or forty-five.

I had been looking down, but as I now turned toward the center of the house, suddenly I stopped dead in my tracks.

In the middle of a doorway stood a white girl, probably a year or so younger than me. She was staring straight at me through big eyes that looked even more afraid than I felt.

The girl wore a long nightgown and some slippers that had bloodstains on them. Her straight blond hair was probably pretty if it was fixed, but now it was all scruffy and matted together. Even from this distance I could tell her eyes were brown. They were so wide they almost looked like they'd been painted on. Her face was whiter than was natural even for a white person. I almost figured her for dead at first, just a dead white girl standing in the middle of the floor like a statue. Her face was just like a ghost. I mean, I'd never seen a ghost, but if I had, I reckon that's what it would look like. She might have been a pretty enough girl in her own way, a little more meat on her than me, but not fat, and three or four inches shorter. Like I said, I was a mite tall and scrawny.

I was still too numb to be surprised. I just looked at her, and she stared back at me. It seemed that everybody else in the whole world was dead. And I figured she'd probably topple over onto the floor any minute with all the rest of the dead people.

We just stood—two silent statues staring at each other.

Then I saw her blink, and the first thing that came to me was that I'd never seen a dead person blink before.

But we just kept standing there staring. I sure enough didn't know what to say.

The white girl with the huge brown eyes and blond hair was the first to speak.

"My . . . my mother is dead," she whimpered, her lips barely moving.

I stood there another few seconds in the trance I'd been in. But somehow the sound of a human voice, and such a pitiful, forlorn sound from a girl who had just said the words that I hadn't wanted to say out loud, finally broke me out of it.

Slowly I found myself walking toward her, stepping through the rubble all around, and not yet even seeing the body that turned out to be her dead daddy in the room behind her. She stood there as I approached, watching me with those huge helpless eyes.

Then suddenly we were in each other's arms, both weeping our eyes out.

FIRST DAY

14

W E STOOD LIKE THAT FOR A WHILE—TEN, MAYBE fifteen seconds—just crying. That doesn't sound like too long, but it's long enough when you're standing in the arms of a complete stranger, especially one with a different color skin.

The awkwardness of it kind of came to us both at the same time, and we slowly stepped away from each other.

After our embrace, neither of us knew what to say. Neither of us could even manage a smile. I realized this girl had met the same fate as I had, though she couldn't know anything yet about the murder of my family.

I reckon I was still numb, still in shock. But it no doubt was a lot worse for her right then. From the look on her face, she must have just found out what had happened, or else had been standing there a long, long time. The bodies were already cold, I could tell that much.

I didn't know what to do. So I just turned and started walking outside.

The white girl must have thought I was leaving. And I reckon I was. This was her house, not mine. Black folks just didn't go into white folks' houses without being invited. I'd forgotten about being hungry.

I'd also forgotten about the dogs. All of a sudden as I walked out the door there came a reddish brown hunting hound running toward me in a full gallop and baying like he'd just cornered a fox or something. On his heels was a light-colored retriever who wasn't making nearly so much noise as the hound, along with a tan collie sprinting up to join in the commotion. All three were barking and howling, sniffing and wagging their tails like dogs do. I guess I must not have smelled too bad since none of them took a chunk out of either of my legs, and after that they treated me like I belonged there.

The girl stood where she was, sniffling and crying for a few more minutes, then found her legs enough to stumble along after me outside. She almost reminded me of a helpless chick following its mother.

I found a shovel from the tool shed and started digging a hole in the ground out in a field some distance from the house.

She made her way up beside me. "What are you doing?" she asked in a trembly voice.

"They gotta be buried," I answered, glancing at her quickly to see if she was going to faint on me.

She just stood there watching blankly. I kept shoveling.

There wasn't a sound anywhere but flies buzzing about, the moo of some cows off someplace nearby, and my shovel scraping into the earth and then tossing the dirt onto a pile next to the hole.

"They your mama and papa?" I said as I shoveled. I watched her out of the corner of my eye. She took a deep breath.

"Yes'm," she finally said. "And my brothers."

"No need to say *yes'm* to me, miss," I said. "I'm just a darkie—a slave from a plantation the other side of Greens Crossing." I'd figured out that much after my wanderings all night.

After a bit the girl turned and walked toward the barn. She returned a minute later dragging another shovel behind her. She stood nearby and tried to dig with me. One look was enough to tell that she'd probably never used a shovel in her life. She didn't even know where to put her hands on the handle or what to do with her foot. But she watched and tried her best to imitate me, managing to scoop out a little dirt.

Side by side we worked on the graves, the final resting places for the white man and woman, the young white man I'd stumbled over outside and another inside the house, which I later found out were the girl's older brothers. The black lady in the house and the two other black folks I'd seen on my way in I figured on burying a little way off from the others. It didn't seem proper that darkies should be buried right by the man and woman who owned the plantation.

Little was said between us as the day went on except what needed saying.

I did most of the digging, which was the way it should have been. I was strong and I didn't mind.

What else did I have to do?

We kept digging on and off for two or three hours. I found the well and fetched us a bucket of water. She didn't drink much, but I did. It was hot. By that time she had bad blisters on her hands. I poured water over them and told her to sit down in the shade and said I'd finish.

I intended to make the holes deeper than I'd done for my family. I knew I'd never finish in one day. But I figured I should be getting the bodies out of the house and over to where we were working. If I had to keep digging tomorrow, as least the girl could sleep in her house tonight. But I didn't think she oughta see what I had to do next.

"Why don't you go for a walk or something," I said.

She looked up at me. "Why?" she said.

"I just think you oughta, that's all. I gotta go get 'em now."

She nodded, stood up and wandered off.

I walked back into the house and wondered how I would get these bodies to the graves all by myself. I looked around and found a small rug. I rolled the girl's mama onto it, then found I could grab hold of the corners and drag it, bit by bit, out of the kitchen and across the yard. I figured her mama'd be the hardest for the girl to have to see, so I wanted to get that body in the ground first. By now it was stiff, and it turned out to be pretty awful work. The blood was dried and black. It was a terrible sight, her eyes open, a look of terror frozen on her white face. I wondered how I had managed to bury my own mama the day before.

It took me more than an hour to drag the bodies to the graves. I dumped one into the deepest hole and covered it with dirt. The black lady was kind of big and took longest, and I almost couldn't do it alone. I thought of calling for the girl to help me with her, but then decided I'd better manage it myself. I'm sorry to say I finally rolled her along the ground instead of dragging her. It seemed awfully undignified, but that was the least of my problems right then.

I put all the bodies next to each other and used another larger rug to cover them up till I could get to them the next day.

I finished just in time to see the white girl walking across a field toward me.

"You likely oughta go in and get dressed," I told her as she approached in her bedraggled nightclothes.

She nodded and went to the house.

She paused and looked back, staring at me a few seconds. She told me later she was already wondering how a girl like me knew how to do so much. With me being colored and a slave, she figured that must explain it.

She was back in a few minutes wearing what looked like a church dress, all pink and frilly with lace. Wasn't the kind of thing I'd have chosen to wear on a day like this. Maybe she didn't have anything else, I didn't know.

By now it was late afternoon. I began to think what to do next. Gradually my brain was picking up speed again. It was already clear to me that this girl I'd run into was completely helpless. I left the graves and went over to meet her.

"You hungry?" I asked as we turned together toward the house.

She nodded.

"I'm near starving," I said. "I ain't had a bite all day. Got anythin' here to eat?"

She shrugged.

I figured I might as well go look. She followed me into the kitchen. There was bread and cheese and eggs. But I didn't feel like making a fire for eggs. So we just had the bread and cheese.

The girl was still in a daze and did whatever I told her, all slow like she was moving through molasses.

We ate and talked a little. Pretty soon it was getting dark. I didn't know how the day'd gone by so fast, but I was glad it was nearly over. From the little I had found out, it was obvious neither of us could do anything else or had any other place to go. She was alone and I was alone, and there we were.

After a while it dawned on me that the cows I'd heard before were bellowing full chisel. I went and looked, and about eight were standing next to the barn, calling out to be milked. So I went and opened the gate to let them in and found buckets and milked them. The girl kept following me about, just watching. At least we now had some warm milk to go with the dry bread and cheese.

By the time I was done, it was full night, and I could tell the girl was about to fall asleep.

We walked back to the house again. I found a lantern and lit it.

"Where's your room?" I asked.

She pointed upstairs.

I walked up the staircase, knowing she'd follow.

"Which one's yours?" I asked, looking around the dark landing.

She pointed to the doorway. I took her hand and led her into it. She lay down on the bed, and I pulled the blanket up over her, then took off her shoes. She didn't seem to think nothing of it. She was asleep in a few minutes.

I figured I ought to stay with her at least for the night. So I found some blankets in another room, settled myself down on the floor a little way from her bed, and blew out the lantern.

That's how I wound up staying the night under the roof of that big plantation house I'd wandered to, my very first in anything but a slave shanty.

Just before I dozed off, I realized we didn't even know each other's names.

WHAT NOW?

15

I RECKON I WAS PRETTY BEAT AND I SLEPT ALL RIGHT, though I came awake a time or two during the night. But I never forgot where I was or how I got there. The reality of what had happened was starting to sink in. My mind didn't play any more tricks on me when I woke up during the night.

I just stared into the darkness, not exactly thinking but reliving it over in my memory. How can you not keep thinking about something so awful as what I'd seen? The look on the face of the dead white lady said it all.

Except for the sound of her gentle breathing, I never heard a peep out of the girl whose room I was in. It didn't seem like she was going to be much help. The thought crossed my mind a time or two that she might be a mite dull. She *looked* normal, but there were occasions when she just didn't seem all there. But then again she'd been through a horrible experience.

It was comforting to hear the sound of another person sleeping nearby, even someone so needy and helpless. I wasn't a girl spooked by every hoot of an owl. But I still felt a heap better hearing another person across the room. If we were the only two people left in the whole world—which was another scary thought I tried to push out of my brain—at least I wasn't completely alone.

I drifted off again and woke up just as the sun was coming up. She was still sound asleep.

I got up quietly and crept out of the room and downstairs. First thing I had to do was go outside and find the necessary. On my way back, I fetched a bucket of water from the well. I didn't know yet that there was a pump inside the kitchen. I'd never even imagined such a contraption. As I carried the bucket inside, I started wondering what to do next.

I had a drink myself and a piece of the bread, which was getting pretty stale by this time. Then I looked around the messy kitchen. I figured the first thing I ought to do was try to clean it up some before the girl got up.

That's when I discovered the water pump and sink. I tried it, pumping a few times till the water started coming out. I just stood staring in amazement. Then I started tidying up the place. I washed the blood as best I could off the floor. I didn't want her to have to see it again. In the other room, where the edge of the rug was all stained from where her papa fell, I just rolled it up. But there was no rug in the kitchen, so I scrubbed the wood floor, though I couldn't get near all the bloodstains out.

I picked up the chairs and started straightening things and cleaning and putting stuff away, or at least setting them on counters or shelves and the table. I found a broom and swept up broken dishes and glass, scooped it up, and put it in a pile outside. When I had the place halfway tidy, I took some time to look around and see what I could see.

It was a pretty big kitchen, with a pantry and larder next to it. There seemed to be plenty of staples—bins of flour, oatmeal, rice, and cornmeal, different kinds of beans, cheeses hanging in the larder. I'd never been inside the kitchen of a rich white man's house, and it sure looked like the girl wouldn't starve anytime soon.

Then I remembered the cows. I heard them starting their hollering to let somebody know their bags were full again.

I went out to the barn, and that's when I realized I was going to have to figure out something to do with all that milk. The buckets from the night before were still sitting there full, with the milk likely getting ready to sour if something wasn't done, and one of them had been knocked over—from a raccoon getting in, from the looks of it.

Right then the cows needed milking, so I just poured the old milk out on the ground outside and started milking them again. As soon as I was done, I let them out to the pasture. The milking didn't take so long this time since they weren't so full as last night. I came back to the kitchen with a bucket of fresh milk. At least we could drink some of it.

By the time the girl came down the stairs, I had a fire in the kitchen stove going. I looked over and there she was standing, staring at me.

I saw from the look on her face that she was going through the same struggle I had the morning before—thinking it must have all been a dream. And now she'd

104

come down to find her dream looking at her from the stove where her mama should have been instead.

I saw those big brown eyes fill with tears. I don't reckon I've ever seen such a wretched, forlorn look in my life. Her hair was still uncombed, and the pink dress she'd put on the day before was full of wrinkles from sleeping in it.

That sight of me caused her whole world—the one that a night's sleep had put back together in her brain—to crumble. If there's any way the second day could be worse than the first, it's from having the reality of the nightmare plunge its knife into your heart all over again. And then it's worse, because you know *for sure* that it's just as bad as you thought. Whatever tiny bit of hope you were clinging to suddenly vanishes in thin air.

So as I said, the sight of me in her mama's kitchen stuck the knife of reality right smack into her heart again.

I walked over to her and once more put my arms around her. She broke down and sobbed like a baby. I don't know what she felt having a rough colored hand in her nice yellow hair, but she didn't seem to mind. I felt like I was comforting one of my little baby sisters. I held her and stroked her hair till I could tell she'd calmed down some.

I stepped back and did my best to smile.

"Sit down," I said, leading her over to the table. "I got a fire going. I'll fix you some eggs."

She obeyed and did what I said.

"Later I'll bake you some fresh bread or maybe

some corn cakes," I said. "Here—have a glass of milk while you're waiting. Then we can go out and gather the mornin's eggs . . . and yesterday's too, I reckon."

She looked up at me and nodded dumbly, then took the glass of milk from my hand and slowly drank a few sips.

"How'd you like a bath after your breakfast?" I asked.

She just kept staring straight ahead.

"I'll boil up lots of warm water. A body feels better after a bath." I was trying to make conversation so she'd get a grip on reality, bad as it was.

"What's your name?" I asked.

"Kathleen," she mumbled in a voice so low I could barely make out the word.

"That what folks call you?"

She nodded.

"Anything else?"

"Katie."

"Katie what?"

"Clairborne."

"Mine's Mary Ann," I said. "Mary Ann Jukes. Folks call me Mayme." I pronounced it *Mame* like my family always had.

If that's how we were finally introduced, there wasn't much to it. Katie didn't actually seem to be paying attention. I could hardly blame her. By now I think I was feeling sorrier for her than for me. I was pretty used to being a big sister.

Katie picked at one egg and a little bit of the leftover bread. It was probably enough, along with the milk, to keep her going for a while.

Me—I ate two fried eggs with some bacon I found, a piece of bread with a hunk of cheese on it and two glasses of milk. In spite of being skinny I knew how to eat. That's one thing my mama always said about me.

I was glad to find that at least my appetite was back. I was going to need all the strength I could find for whatever lay ahead.

MOVIN' ON

16

I HELPED KATIE WITH A BATH AND DID MY BEST TO wash her hair, let it dry, and fix it nice. It felt funny after never feeling any but colored hair in my life. Hers was long and soft and light and moved around easy in my hands like I imagined silk would feel, though I'd never seen or felt silk either. But I didn't say anything to Katie about what I was thinking. I just tried to fix it how I'd seen white girls wear their hair.

A person always feels fresher after a bath and clean clothes. I think Katie did too, though she still hadn't smiled. Not that I expected her to. Who'd be able to smile after what she'd been through? But I was trying to get her to feel better and start thinking for herself before I had to leave.

While she was finishing up and getting dressed, I told her that I was going out to finish the burying and to stay inside till I was done. Then I went out and got back to work on the graves. My arms were plumb wore out from yesterday, but the holes had to be deeper and I knew I had to finish it today.

I spent the whole morning at it and was dog tired when I was through. But finally I got each body in the ground maybe about three feet, which I figured was enough, and covered with dirt.

When I was done I stood there and said the Lord's Prayer over them. Seemed like something that ought to be done. Then I took a deep breath and said, "God, take care of 'em."

Then I found myself a wooden tub and washed myself real good.

I knew I couldn't stay much longer. This was a white man's plantation, and a colored girl like me had no call to be sleeping here and eating their food and all. I figured Katie must have other kin that'd come for her by and by. When that time came, the best place for me to be was good and gone, else they'd likely think I had something to do with the tragedy. So I was thinking it was about time for me to be heading on. But I wanted to do what I could, with Katie so helpless, to get her through the first few days till whoever it was came for her.

The rest of that day I tried to clean up the main floor of the house as best I could, with her making stabs at trying to help. By that second night it was mostly put back together, though I couldn't do anything about the broken windows. I also made a batch of bread to make sure Katie'd have enough to eat for a while after I left.

She lingered nearby as I worked, pitching in sometimes or just watching. I had to get her to help lift the dish cabinet and some bookshelves because they were too heavy for me to lift all by myself. She wasn't too strong, but we managed to get them back upright. Most of the glassware was broken. The few things that weren't, I put away again.

Then there were the books. There were more books in that house than I'd ever imagined could be anywhere. How could one family have so many books? I thought it would be awfully nice to be smart enough to read books like these.

As I started putting them back on the shelves, I just stuck them in any which way. Katie, who'd been watching me absently, now came over and started rearranging them, turning some of them over and taking some out and putting them somewhere else, and collecting different ones together with others. She seemed to know where every single one had been before. Sometimes she'd stop and look at one of them a few seconds, maybe turning over a few pages and looking inside. I could tell she loved them.

"You can read these?" I asked as I picked up another pile from the floor and brought them over to the shelf.

"Some of them" was all she said. She was holding one with a few pictures in it, and now walked over and sat down on one of the chairs and started reading it. I kept taking the ones from the floor and stacking them on the shelves. I thought anything to distract her mind for a spell was a good thing, and I was glad she'd found a book she liked.

For the rest of the day Katie helped me and read, took a couple of naps, and cried a few times. When we were cleaning up and she picked up her broken violin, the tears poured down her cheeks. I could tell it was really special to her, and we didn't throw it away like the broken dishes.

Every once in a while Katie would disappear for an hour or so. Then suddenly I'd see her a little ways off staring at me again. I didn't quite know what to make of it. She didn't say a word unless I asked her a question.

One thing I started to be curious about was the Clairbornes' slaves. Why hadn't anybody come around—white *or* colored? That's when I realized their slaves must have been killed too. And were those two women I'd buried the day before the only house slaves? I thought maybe I ought to have another look around. I didn't want poor Katie stumbling over any more dead bodies.

But I didn't find anyone in the main house or anyplace nearby. And I didn't feel too inclined to wander off and look for the Clairbornes' colored quarters. I knew if anybody found me doing what I was doing, I'd be in so much trouble I didn't even want to think about it.

When night came I helped Katie into bed and slept on her floor again.

The next morning I got up, made a fire, milked the cows, and got things as ready for Katie as I could. She came downstairs, looking a little like she was starting to get used to the notion of what things were like. I fixed us breakfast and ate as much as I could myself, since I figured it'd have to last me a good spell.

I didn't have anything to pack since I'd come with nothing, but I did stick one of the loaves of bread I'd made under my arm. Then I turned to Katie, who was sitting at the kitchen table.

"Well," I said, "I reckon you'll be okay now, Miss Katie. You got bread and plenty of food to last you. Just make sure you keep the cows milked so they don't dry up."

"I can't milk a cow," she said, just staring at me.

"I reckon you'll have to learn, then," I said. " 'Cause it's time for me to be saying good-bye."

She looked at me with a confused expression. Then it slowly changed to horror. Her eyes got wide like she'd heard the most awful thing in the world.

"Why . . . *why* are you saying good-bye?" she whispered, then a little sob followed.

"I gotta go," I said.

"Go," she repeated, as if the idea hadn't ever occurred to her. "Why . . . go where?"

"I don't know. Just go."

"But . . . you can't . . . *leave!*" she said.

All at once something dawned on me I hadn't thought of before. She probably figured all this time that I was one of the Clairborne slaves.

"I ain't one of your daddy's coloreds, Miss Katie," I said.

"Why are you here, then?" she asked.

" 'Cause my family got killed too."

"Oh," she said. "But . . . but you can't . . ."

"This ain't my place."

"*Please* don't go."

The panic in her voice stabbed at my heart, but I didn't know what else to say. I turned and walked outside, still holding the loaf of bread. I had to think. Just when I had got my mind made up, all of a sudden I was confused all over again about what to do.

Then I heard a voice behind me.

"Colored girl . . ."

I turned around. There was Katie standing in the doorway.

"—please . . . come back," she whimpered.

As she spoke I could see her eyes glistening with tears.

"I don't want you to go away," she said, then hesitated. A funny look came over her face, a more expressive one than I'd yet seen.

"I'm . . . I'm sorry," she added, "—I forgot your name."

"Mayme," I said.

"Please . . . Mayme," she said, "—I'm afraid. Can't you stay a little longer with me? I need you to help me. I don't know what to do."

Now it was *my* turn to stand there staring at her. After a while I moved back toward the house. She smiled a kind of nervous half smile. I knew it was her way of thanking me for not leaving.

I smiled back.

Then together we walked into the kitchen.

Routine and a New Bed

17

I STILL KNEW I'D HAVE TO LEAVE SOMETIME. A girl like Katie *had* to have some friends or kinfolk who would come for her any day. It was a mite curious to me why we hadn't seen another living soul all this time—no neighbors, nobody. I'd been pretty nervous that somebody'd see me traipsing around so familiar-like inside a big plantation house. But the fact was, until somebody came, Katie had to learn a few things, since eventually I'd have to go.

That same evening I tried to teach her to milk the cows. That was some chore!

Watching her tiptoeing around, trying to keep her feet out of the manure, and then grimacing as she put her hand on one of the cow's teats like it was going bite her or something, I could hardly keep myself from laughing out loud.

"Ugh!" she exclaimed, snatching her hand back.

"Ain't nothin' to be afraid of, Miss Katie," I said after I got hold of myself. "It's just a cow—ain't gonna hurt you."

"But it feels so . . . funny. And it smells bad in here."

"Just the smell of a barn."

Finally she sat down on the stool and tried to squeeze out some milk.

"Nothing's coming out," she said.

"You gotta squeeze hard and pull down at the same time," I said. "Like this."

I showed her how to do it, and a stream of milk hit the bottom of the bucket.

"Now you try it again," I said.

We switched places and she put her hand out and tried it again.

Finally a little dribble trickled out.

"That's it, Miss Katie. You done good. Now, just keep at it while I go milk the others."

When we were done, she'd managed to get the cow's bag about halfway empty and, I think, felt some satisfaction about it. I doubt she'd ever done anything like it before. She seemed to perk up a bit after that and kept wanting to help from then on.

The next day we got more of the house put back together, making the kitchen and parlor look pretty normal and probably about like they had been. It was the biggest, nicest house I'd ever been in, and it felt good to get it into shape. We also picked up some of the broken things from outside. Luckily, no major damage was done, so that after a couple of days the outside of the house looked presentable too.

Every once in a while I'd catch myself and think, *What in tarnation you doing, Mayme, you fool colored girl, moving things around and acting like it's your own place?*

But then I'd take one look at Katie and remember that if I didn't help her, it didn't seem like anybody would.

She was able to help a little more and began to talk some. By the third or fourth day, we were sort of finding ourselves a routine—getting up, fixing a fire, milking the cows and collecting the eggs, then having breakfast and cleaning up and planning what we needed to do for that day to have enough to eat for the rest of it.

I usually got up first and made the fire and started with the cows. By and by she'd wander outside to the barn with her boots on, still looking sleepy. Whether she really wanted to help or was still a little afraid to be alone, it didn't matter to me. She was doing the best she was able, and was starting to earn my respect.

I didn't mind the work. But it was nice when she tried to help too. Gradually the firewood in the kitchen ran out, so we had to haul more from the woodpile out by the barn. There was plenty to do. The days seemed to go by fast enough.

Every two or three days I'd bake some bread. I finally got the churn going and made some fresh butter from the cream to go on our bread. We drank what milk we could and gave some to the cats and dogs. But until we started making cheese, there was too much to use, and I still had to pour lots of it out.

I was pretty familiar by this time with the whole place and the pantry and kitchen and all the rest. There was plenty to eat for now. But I could see plain enough that even for only two girls like us it wouldn't last forever. The flour was sure to run out eventually. Of course I didn't think too much about that on account of I still figured to be gone before long with

Katie being taken care of by her own people.

I wasn't thinking of anything but each day as it came, one at a time. How long I'd stay—I didn't think about. Another couple of days, maybe three or four. I wasn't the kind of person who planned my life out. I'd never needed to. I always just did as I was told. This was the first time in my life I had to think ahead about what to do.

For those first few days I kept sleeping on the floor in Katie's room. But then one night came when we were getting ready for bed, and Katie asked, "Why don't you sleep in a bed?"

I looked at her, puzzled at first.

"'Cause there's only one bed in the room," I said, "and that's yours."

"I mean one of the other beds."

"The floor suits me fine."

"But it's so hard. Why would you want to sleep on the floor? Why don't you sleep in . . . my brother's room?"

I stared at her a moment, not sure I'd heard her right.

"I can't do that," I finally said.

"Why not?" she asked.

"'Cause, Miss Katie, I'm colored."

The strangest look came over her face, just for an instant, almost like she'd forgotten our skins were different.

"Oh . . ." she said, as if my reluctance at last made sense. "But . . . I don't think of you as colored," she said. "And I want you to sleep in a bed. I'm sure you'll sleep better."

"You *want* me to?" I said.

She nodded. I hardly even realized at first what a big thing that was, her making a statement like that. She'd made a decision, taken initiative, by saying something she *wanted* me to do. It was pretty amazing when I thought about it. Up till that time I almost didn't know if she could think for herself at all. I was real glad to see that she could.

"You won't be afraid in here all by yourself?" I said.

"You can come in again if I get afraid."

"All right," I said. "I reckon I can try it."

So I did—that same night. It sure enough was a huckleberry above a persimmon to anyplace I'd slept in. It was the softest, nicest bed I'd ever felt.

I didn't sleep so good at first. All I could think was that I was in a white man's bed, and if anyone found me I'd be in for it bad. But after another couple of nights, I started to sleep pretty sound.

After that Katie called it my room. I was a little nervous about that. But I didn't figure there'd be any harm for another few days.

NEIGHBORLY CALL

18

THE NEXT DAY, ABOUT THE MIDDLE OF THE MORNING, I was on my way back from the chicken coop with some fresh eggs when I heard the dogs start barking. I looked up and saw a white man on a horse coming toward the house along the wagon road that came from the west.

My heart jumped into my throat and I ran for the house. Katie was inside kneading some bread we'd mixed up earlier.

"There's a man coming, Miss Katie!" I called as I hurried through the kitchen. "Come with me!"

I didn't even stop but ran through and up the stairs, with Katie following me, her hands all caked with flour and bits of dough. A minute later we knelt down and peeked over the edge of the window in the direction of the road.

"It's Mr. Thurston," said Katie after she'd had a look.

"Who's he?" I asked.

"A neighbor. He's a friend of my daddy's. He owns a plantation too."

"Where?"

"I don't know—two or three miles from here I think."

I tried to think for a minute. He was almost to the house by now, the three dogs yapping and running around his horse.

"You go down and see what he wants," I said after a few seconds.

"What should I say?" asked Katie nervously.

"I don't know . . . you'll have to see what he wants. Is he somebody who can help you?"

"I . . . I don't know." Katie's voice faltered and she looked scared. "I don't know what to do—"

"Shouldn't you tell him what happened?"

"I don't think so—"

"Who's your kin?" I interrupted again.

"I don't know . . . Uncle Templeton and Uncle Burchard, I guess."

"Do you want to go live with either of them?"

A look came over her face that said clearly enough what the answer was.

"Then I reckon we gotta talk later about what to do and what's to become of you," I said. "But right now you gotta see what he wants."

"Mr. Thurston's a nice man. He wouldn't do anything to us." I could tell Katie was trying to sound confident, but I wasn't so sure.

"He might not do anything to you," I told her, "but he ain't about to think well of a colored girl living in your house. He'd tell somebody, and then they'd come and—"

A knock on the door downstairs cut off what I was about to say. Katie's eyes got big as plates.

"Go on . . . you got to," I said. "Tell him as little as

you can. If he sees me, maybe he'll think I'm your mama's house slave. Go on, Miss Katie. He's gonna start wondering pretty soon."

Another knock sounded on the door, a little louder this time.

Slowly Katie got up and walked out of the room toward the stairs. I crept after her and stopped at the landing so I could hear what they said.

I heard the door open.

"Hello, Mr. Thurston," Katie said, her voice shaking a little.

"Good morning, Miss Kathleen," said a man's voice. It sounded friendly enough. "I was beginning to think no one was here. Is your mama home?"

"No, sir. She's . . . uh, she's not here."

"I didn't see any of the slaves out anywhere."

"They must be out in the fields. Mama saw to everything before she left."

"Hmm . . . all right, then. I just came by to see how she was getting on after all that ruckus last week with Bilsby's bunch. You all doing fine?"

"Yes, sir."

"Well, I heard they caught and killed a few of 'em on the other side of Greens Crossing, though Bilsby got away. Any word from your daddy when he'll be coming home?"

"No, sir."

"Well, can't be too much longer, I reckon.—All right, then, Miss Kathleen, you tell your mama I was here and to let me know if she needs anything."

"Thank you, Mr. Thurston."

I heard the door close. Quickly I went back to the window and peeked out. The man was walking toward his horse, though real slow and looking around every now and then. I couldn't see his face, but I had the feeling he was turning some things over in his mind about what Katie'd said, as well as maybe wondering why the place didn't look as tidy as usual. Luckily most of the broken windows were on the other side of the house. But he kept going, got on his horse and rode away.

I heard Katie's footsteps behind me. I turned around.

"You did real good, Miss Katie."

"I didn't actually lie to him, did I, Mayme?" she asked.

"No, Miss Katie, that wasn't really lying," I said, though I felt a mite uncertain about the whole thing myself.

"Maybe he could have helped us like you said," Katie went on.

"He might have helped you, Miss Katie. But the only help he'd have given me would be to take me as his own slave, or something worse. But who else you got for kin, Miss Katie? If you don't want to live with those two uncles, who would they give you to?"

"I don't know. There's my daddy's brother Burchard I told you about."

"Where's he live?"

"Someplace on the other side of Charlotte. But it's kind of a long ways away. We didn't see them very often."

"Does he have a big plantation like this?"

"I think so."

"Your mama—she got any kin?"

"She has a sister up North somewhere, my aunt Nelda. But I've never seen her. Mama says her family wasn't too happy about her marrying a Southerner."

"Who's that other fella you said?"

"Uncle Templeton. He's my mother's brother—but Mama doesn't—didn't seem to like him much. And Uncle Ward too."

"Who's he?"

"My mama's other brother, but I think he's dead. Mama talked about him like he was. Uncle Templeton used to come around, but he and Mama would always argue. Last time he was here, he stole Mama's money."

"When was that?"

"A while, maybe a year ago."

Talking to Katie about her kin didn't get us much nearer knowing what to do.

INVESTIGATION

19

TALKING ABOUT KATIE'S AUNT AND THREE UNCLES got me to thinking about a lot of things. I wondered what kind of people they were, whether they'd come to take Katie when they found out what had happened. It seemed to me like she had to do something to try to get in touch with one of them.

"You really oughta find out more about your kin," I said to Katie the next day. "You need to decide what you're gonna do."

I didn't know if Katie realized how serious it all was. I was surprised to find out the next morning that she'd been paying more attention than I'd realized.

I heard papers shuffling when I woke up. I got out of bed and walked out into the hallway. In a small library next to her mama and daddy's bedroom, Katie was in her nightgown seated at a big desk on the far wall with the top rolled up.

"It's my daddy's secretary," she said when she heard me walk up behind her. "This was his office. Mama used it after he left."

There were papers everywhere, in stacks and drawers and cubbyholes, and a couple of sets of keys on rings.

"I thought about what you said," Katie went on.

"I'm worried about what would happen if Uncle Templeton came back. So I thought I would look through here and see if I could learn anything about him."

"Find anything?" I asked.

"There's a letter here from my mama's brother Ward, written from California."

"When from?"

She showed it to me. It was dated 1852.

"That's thirteen years ago," I said. "You and I were barely born back then. Lots could have changed since. What does it say?"

She took the letter and read a little of it out loud. The handwriting was as bad as mine if I had tried to write a letter like that. It looked like hen scratching.

Me and some other fellas, it said, *think we hit a vein, Sis. If it pans out, I'll git you everything you ever wanted.*

I looked at Katie. "You ever hear any more about this?" I asked.

Katie shook her head.

She put the letter down. "Anything else?" I asked.

"There's this funeral announcement about Aunt Nelda's husband from Philadelphia."

"You know him?"

"No. Mama hardly ever talked about them, and we never saw them."

"What about that fellow Templeton you were talking about?"

"I don't think he's the kind that writes letters," said Katie.

"And the other man, the one who you said had a

plantation someplace?"

"My daddy's brother Burchard—no, I haven't seen anything about him either. Do you think it's okay if I keep looking through my mama's stuff?"

"Yeah, I do," I said. "Seems likely one of 'em's the one you'll have to go stay with. Likely enough your mama and daddy's plantation and this house and all the land, and maybe you too, belongs to one or the other of them—this place has gotta belong to somebody of your kin now that your mama and daddy's gone. Seems like it'd be good if you knew which one. Likely as not it's your daddy's kin, probably that man with a plantation of his own."

Everything I said seemed to sober Katie pretty good. I don't think it had completely dawned on her yet that the time was coming, sure as night followed day, that she'd have to go live with somebody else. I couldn't see any other way it could be.

I sure didn't know what would happen to me, but that's what was likely to happen to Katie. Maybe things would work out and they'd let her keep me for her own slave.

Though my experience told me not to let myself hope for that too much.

SPECIAL DAY

20

I DIDN'T WANT TO MAKE HER NERVOUS AGAIN, SO I didn't bring up Katie's kin for a few more days. I figured it was something she needed to do, and in a way it wasn't none of my affair—just as long as I was gone before anyone found *me* here. But Katie didn't seem all that inclined to do much about it, which puzzled me some.

Then what she said one morning showed me how little she was thinking about what was going to become of her.

"Can we bake a cake?" Katie asked me while we were eating breakfast.

"I reckon . . . sure," I said. "Why do you want a cake?"

"I just feel like having cake," she answered. "It's my birthday, and Mama always made me a cake."

She looked away and started to cry.

"Oh, Miss Katie," I said. "I'm sorry."

I walked over to her, hesitated a few seconds, then took one of her hands between the two of mine. She glanced up at me and wiped her eyes with her other hand.

"I want my mama," she wept. "I can't stand it at night when I remember what happened. Sometimes I think I'm just going to die from being so sad."

"I'm so sorry, Miss Katie," I said. "I can't make it go away, and I don't reckon there's much of anything I can do to make you happier. But it's going to be all right. You and me are going to make out all right. We'll get through this somehow."

She sniffed and rubbed the back of her hand across her eyes again.

"Your skin," she said, "it feels the same as mine . . . only a little rougher—like my daddy's."

"That's just from the work," I told her. "Skin is skin, whether it's brown or white, it's still the same."

She reached out and touched my head, then smiled kind of sheepish-like.

"But hair's not the same, is it?" I said, smiling back.

She shook her head.

"Mine's wound in tight little curls, and yours is straight and soft."

"I was curious what it felt like," she said. "I've never felt colored hair before."

Katie held my hand a few seconds longer, like she was thinking, then slowly let it go.

"Can I feel yours again?" I asked. I remembered how smooth it felt the day I washed it.

"My what?" she asked.

"Your hair. It's so soft and silky."

"I don't mind," she said.

I reached out and slowly ran my fingers through her hair, then drew my hand back and giggled. I couldn't help it. We both laughed.

"Happy birthday, Miss Katie," I said after we were quiet again.

"Thank you," she replied.

"I wish I had something for you."

"That's all right. You didn't know. It won't be the same without my mama, but I'm glad you're here with me. If you'll show me how to make a cake, that will be enough."

"Then let's go see what there is in the pantry and get started.—How old are you today?"

"Fifteen."

"That makes you as old as me," I replied. "For a while, at least. I'll turn sixteen at the end of the summer."

We set about making the cake right away. It wasn't anything fancy. Any cakes I'd had in my life had been few and far between. But I had something of an idea what to do, and we found a recipe in a book of Katie's mama's. I wanted to think of something special to do for Katie's birthday, but all I could come up with was a stew made with some beef jerky from the pantry.

I was working on it in the kitchen, with water boiling on top of the stove as I was tossing things into it, and the nice smell from the baking cake was starting to fill up the house. I heard a sound coming from the parlor—like singing but not quite the same. I put down my knife and wiped my hands and went in. There was Katie sitting at the piano. It was the first time I'd ever heard piano music.

"That sounds awfully pretty, Miss Katie," I said after listening for a minute. It reminded me of evenings around the campfire and everyone singing our favorite songs. "I didn't know you could play so good."

"Mama taught me, along with the violin," she said. "You should hear her play. She's real good. She plays Chopin—"

She stopped and took a deep breath.

"She used to, I mean," she added.

"Well, that's the best music I ever heard," I said, trying to sound cheerful. "Keep playing, Miss Katie. I'll listen while I'm making your birthday stew."

I went back into the kitchen and finished cutting up a few vegetables we'd found in the garden. I reckon there's something special about music that gets under your skin—black, white, brown . . . any kind of skin. Music can make you sad, or it can make you happy. Katie had a music book in front of her and was playing from it. It had such a happy sound that it couldn't help but liven up our spirits.

"That's so nice, Miss Katie," I repeated when I joined her again. "I've never heard such pretty music. We used to sing a lot in the evenings, but there weren't any pianos, and mostly no instruments at all, just voices. It was pretty enough. But what you're playing is so different than anything I ever heard."

"That was Mozart," she said.

"What does that mean?" I asked.

"Mozart—he's the composer who wrote it."

"Oh. Who's he? It's a funny name."

"He was a man who lived in Vienna," Katie answered. "He was born about a hundred years ago.

He wrote sonatas and dances and operas and all kinds of songs."

"I've never heard of any of those kinds of things. Where's Vienna?" I asked.

"In Austria."

"Well, all I know is that it's mighty fine. It makes you feel like dancing a jig."

Katie laughed.

"What's funny?" I said, laughing with her.

"You don't dance a jig to Mozart," she said. "You dance a minuet."

"A min-you-what?"

She laughed again.

"A minuet. I was playing one of Mozart's country dances. A jig is fast, a minuet is slow and graceful."

She played the little tune again.

"See . . . like that," she said. "I'll show you."

She got up from the piano stool and danced a few steps around the room, so light and delicate as she lifted up and down from her toes. She looked like a princess or something.

"That's real pretty," I said.

Katie went back to the piano and played the melody again, then came back and stood in front of me.

"Take my hands," she said. "I'll teach it to you."

"I could never do it like you did!" I said.

"Sure you can . . . here, we'll do it together."

She started to sing the melody she had just been playing on the piano. Not really *sing* it, because there were no words. But she hummed the notes, kind of like *dum-dee-dee-dum-dee-dum,* and then she started stepping slowly back and forth, holding on to my hands and leading me as she went.

"Just do what I do," she told me.

I tried to imitate her but felt like a brambling cow alongside her graceful steps.

"All right, do that little part again . . ." she said, and we started over.

". . . then turn slowly around," she said, letting go of my hands.

I kept watching and tried to imitate her. After three or four tries I started to be able to do it a little better.

"That's good, Mayme!" she said. "Now you do that part again while I play it on the piano. See if you can remember it and do it in time to the music."

She went back to the piano, got ready to play, then gave me a little nod with her head. I did what she'd taught me in step with the music. By now I could feel the rhythm of it a little better and went through the whole thing as she played.

"That was good!" she exclaimed. "Let's dance it together again. Then I'll show you the next stanza. You can help me sing now. Here's how the next part goes."

She played it two or three times, then came back to show me what to do next.

After another fifteen or twenty minutes, I had learned it and we had danced the whole thing together.

"That was fun, Miss Katie," I said. "I've never heard that kind of music before in my life. It's real nice."

"What kind of music did you have where you lived?"

"I don't know—what's called colored music, I reckon."

"What's it like?"

"Just singing," I said, "sometimes with a fiddle or a banjo, but mostly singing and clapping with all the men and women singing lots of harmony."

"Will you teach me a song, Mayme?"

I couldn't help chuckling at the thought of Katie singing a colored field chant, or rocking back and forth clapping and wailing to a camp meeting revival chorus.

"What's so funny about that?" she wanted to know. "If you can learn the minuet, why can't I learn your music?"

"All right," I said. "Let me see . . . I'll sing you a revival song."

"What's that?"

"A song we sing when we go to religious meetings."

"You mean church?"

"Not exactly, but a little like it, I reckon. When the white folks are having their camp meeting in a big tent, we have a colored revival out in the field."

I started clapping first, and rocking a little to get myself into the rhythm, then started singing.

"Oh, whar shill we go w'en de great day comes,
Wid de blowin' er de trumpits en de bangin' er de
    drums?
How many po' sinners'll be kotched out late
En fine no latch ter de golden gate?"

"I can hardly understand a word you're saying," Katie laughed. "It's like Beulah and Elvia sounded when they talked fast to each other."

"Who's that?"

"My mama's house slaves. They're the ones . . . the ones you buried that day you came."

That quieted us for a minute. How strange it was that we'd been singing—almost like we'd forgotten for a few minutes what had happened.

"Anyhow, that's the way we coloreds sing it," I said after a bit.

"Teach me the words," said Katie. "I want to sing it with you."

I repeated it line by line with her a couple of times.

"Then this is the chorus," I said.

"No use fer ter wait twel ter-morrer!
De sun musn't set on yo' sorrer,
Sin's ez sharp ez a bamboo brier—
Oh, Lord! fetch de mo'ners up higher!"

"And you gotta clap and sway in time to the music," I said.

She tried it as we sang the first verse and chorus again, but she couldn't quite get the rhythm right. I couldn't help laughing, but then we tried it again.

After a while we were singing pretty good together, and I even tried a little harmony alongside her voice on the melody. Then I taught her the next verse, and we stumbled through it together, and then a third time.

"W'en de nashuns er de earf is a stan'in all
  aroun',
Who's a gwineter be choosen fer ter w'ar de glory-
  crown?
Who's a gwine fer ter stan' stiff-kneed en bol'.
En answer to der name at de callin' er de roll?
You better come now ef you comin'—
Ole Satun is loose en a bummin'—
De wheels er distruckshun is a hummin'—
Oh, come 'long, sinner, ef you comin'!"

By now Katie was gradually getting the feel of the song, though she still couldn't say the words like an old black man would say them. Then we sang the last two verses, and she was clapping in time with the best of them.

When we were finished, we fell down on the sofa, laughing like we'd never laughed before.

"I don't see how you can remember all that," said Katie as we rested.

"I've heard it fifty times," I said. "Every word's stuck in my brain. You did real good for your first time."

"You did good with the dancing too."

"It was fun, Miss Katie," I said. "There sure are lots of different kinds of music. I've never danced like that before."

"I haven't danced the minuet since before the war," she said slowly. "Mama and Daddy used to go dancing. Sometimes they'd take me with them. But after the war came, everything changed."

"Well, we'll dance again after your birthday supper.
We'll call it Miss Katie Clairborne's birthday
minuet."

She laughed again, and it was good to see. I was
glad she could be a little bit happy on her birthday.

"I can smell the cake already," she said, then paused
and looked over at me. "Thank you, Mayme, for
making this a special day for me."

BOOKS, DOLLS, AND BEDTIME STORIES

21

AN EVENING OR TWO LATER I CAME UPON KATIE
sitting on her bed with a book in her lap.

"What's that about?" I asked.

"A foolish little girl named Rosamond."

"Why is she foolish?"

"Because she is very poor and needs new shoes, but
she wants a purple jar instead. And her mother lets her
have her choice between the shoes and the vase. Rosamond chooses the vase but soon sees what a foolish
choice she has made. Then she has to wait a whole
month for new shoes."

"What's it called?"

"*The Purple Jar*," answered Katie.

"Would you read it to me?"

"Here, you can borrow it and read it yourself."

"I'm not that good a reader. I've never read a book like that before."

"It's so much better to read it to yourself."

"My mama only taught me to read a little. We didn't have any books."

"Why?"

"We were slaves, Miss Katie. We was poor as Job's turkey. We didn't have no money for things like books."

The idea of not having money or books seemed new to her.

"Where did you live?" she asked.

"From here, I'm not sure exactly. Over yonder somewhere." I waved toward the east.

"All you have to do to learn to read better is to read more," said Katie. "You can ask me about the words you don't know. You're smart, Mayme. You're about the smartest person I know—except for my mama."

"I don't know anything about the kinds of things you know about," I said. "You know about books and music and places like the town where that Mozart man lived."

"But you can *do* things, Mayme. That makes you smart in a different way. And sometimes I get confused and afraid . . . and then I don't know what to do."

"Everybody gets afraid, Miss Katie."

"I've never seen you afraid."

"I get afraid all the time. I was terrified out of my wits when those men killed my family, probably the same men that came here, those marauders like that neighbor fella said. I was plenty scared. And I'm still scared sometimes, when I'm lying awake in your brother's bed and hearing noises, and I remember that it's just me and you here, and I think what they'll do to me if anyone finds me like this. And I start worrying about rape or getting murdered myself, and then I get so afraid I can't stand it."

"What's rape, Mayme?"

"Something you don't need to know about, Miss Katie. Let's just hope it don't ever happen to you or me. But let's don't talk about that any more. I want you to read to me from that book."

"If you just try, Mayme, I know you could read it yourself in no time."

"All right, I'll try," I said. "But for now, why don't you read me some from it . . . to help me get started."

"All right. Here, come and sit on the bed with me.— Wait, let me get my dolls!" she exclaimed.

She ran over to her dresser and grabbed two, then picked up two more from the foot of the bed. When she came back and sat down next to me, she had several dolls under each arm. She arranged them beside her on the bed.

"This is Peg," she said, "and Missie . . . and Sarah . . . and Rebecca . . . and Jane. Would you like to have one of them, Mayme?"

"I, uh . . . I don't—no, Miss Katie," I said. "They're yours. I don't—"

"But I want you to have one," she said. "Here—I want you to have Rebecca. Her skin is white, but you like people with white skin, don't you, Mayme?"

I smiled. "Yes, Miss Katie," I said. "I like folks with white skin."

"Good, then from now on, Rebecca is yours."

"But, Miss Katie," I said, "she looks like she's the most costly one of them all."

"I don't know about that. Mama and Daddy got these dolls for me in Charleston. They were all birthday presents. So now since it was my birthday two days ago, I'm making a present to you."

"I . . . I don't . . . all right, Miss Katie," I said. "That's about the nicest thing anybody's ever done for me. I don't know what to say." I looked over at her. "Thank you, Miss Katie," I said. "This is something I won't ever forget."

"Now let's read," said Katie.

She picked up another book lying next to her, arranged it in her lap, then opened it to the first page. I looked at it over her shoulder. She pointed to the words, probably for my benefit.

"'Alice was beginning to get very tired of sitting by her sister on the bank, and of having nothing to do,'" Katie began. "'Once or twice she had peeped into the book her sister was reading, but it had no pictures or conversations in it, "and what is the use of a book," thought Alice, "without pictures or conversations?"'"

"Who's Alice?" I asked.

"I don't know," replied Katie. "I've never read this book before. It's new. My mother got it for me only last month."

"What's it called?"

"*Alice's Adventures in Wonderland*."

"That sounds interesting," I said. "Read some more."

Katie picked up the book again and continued on. "'So she was considering,'" she read, "'in her own mind (as well as she could, for the hot day made her feel very sleepy and stupid), whether the pleasure of making a daisy-chain would be worth the trouble of getting up and picking the daisies, when suddenly a White Rabbit with pink eyes ran close by her.'"

Katie continued the story, her fingers following along the page, and I listened until Alice had fallen down the rabbit hole and was beginning to have all kinds of strange adventures.

After Katie had read several chapters, she put the book down and lay back on her pillows.

"I'm sleepy," she sighed.

"Would you like to *hear* a story," I asked, "like I used to tell my brothers and sisters?"

"You had brothers and sisters?"

"A whole houseful."

"What's happened to them?"

"They all got killed."

The thought seemed to sober Katie. It was quiet a minute.

"I'm sorry, Mayme," she said after a bit. "I forget sometimes that you lost your family too. But, please— yes, I would like to hear a story."

"One that I made up or one that the old slave folks tell the young'uns everywhere?"

"Anything you like, Mayme. You choose."

"All right—let me see . . . I think I'll tell you about the fox and little rabbits."

"Is it scary—he won't eat them, will he?"

"You will have to wait and see. That's just what I used to tell Samuel all the time—wait and see.—Do you want me to tell it like my grandpapa would say it to us?"

"You mean with the words sounding funny?"

"Just like my grandpapa talked."

"Yes, I want to hear it like he told it."

Katie leaned back and got comfortable.

"Well dar wuz a certain rabbit who'll we'll jist call Mr. Rabbit," I began. "En Mr. Rabbit's chilluns, dey minded der daddy en mammy fum day's een' ter day's een'."

A little giggle came from Katie.

"You sound funny, Mayme," she said, giggling again.

"You said you wanted me to make it sound like my grandpapa."

"I do," said Katie. "Keep going."

"Well," I went on, "as I was saying, Mr. Rabbit's chilluns, dey was good chilluns. W'en ole man Rabbit say 'scoot,' dey scooted, en w'en ole Mrs. Rabbit say 'scat,' dey scatted. Dey did dat. En dey kep der cloze clean, en dey ain't had no smut on der nose nudder. En ef dey hadn't er bin good chilluns, der wuz one time w'en dey wouldn't er bin no little rabbits—na'er one. Dat's w'at. Do you want to know w'en dat time was?"

"Yes, when was it?" said Katie. So I went on to explain that it was the time when Mr. Fox dropped in

140

at Mr. Rabbit's house and didn't find anyone except the little rabbits. Old Mr. Rabbit was off somewhere raiding a collard patch, and old Mrs. Rabbit was attending a quilting in the neighborhood. While the little rabbits were playing hide-and-switch, in drops Mr. Fox. The little rabbits were so fat they fairly make his mouth water, but he remembered Mr. Wolf, and he was afraid to gobble them up unless he got some real good reason.

"What happened to Mr. Wolf?" asked Katie in a sleepy voice.

"Mr. Wolf, he come roun' to Mr. Rabbit's too, en he weren't too smart. En Mr. Rabbit tricked him, en locked him into his wood chist, en den poured boilin' water in on him en killed him dead. En so Mr. Fox, he's wary ob Mr. Rabbit. En de little rabbits, dey mighty skittish, en dey sorter huddle deyse'f up tergedder en watch Mr. Fox. En Mr. Fox, he sit der en study w'at sorter skuse he gwineter make up so's he kin eat der little rabbits. Bimeby he see a great big stalk er sugarcane stan'in up in de corner, and he clear up his throat en say: 'Yer! you young rabs dar, come roun' yer en break me a piece er dat sweetnin'-tree en bring it to me,' sezee.

"De little rabbits, dey got out de sugarcane, dey did, en dey rastle wid it, en sweat over it, but twan't no use. Dey couldn't break it. Mr. Fox, he make like he ain't watchin', but he keep on holler'n: 'Hurry up dar, rabs! I'm a waitin' on you.'

"En de little rabbits, dey hustle roun' en rastle wid it some more, but dey couldn't break it. Bimeby dey hear little bird singin' on top er de house, en de song w'at de little bird sing wuz dish yer:

> *" 'Take yo' toofies en gnyaw it,*
> *Take yo' toofies en saw it,*
> *Saw it en yoke it,*
> *En den you kin broke it.' "*

And so it went as I told the story, thinking about my grandpapa and my family as the familiar story rolled off my tongue.

I finally came to, "But Mr. Fox, he knows what happen to Mr. Wolf, so he button up his coat collar tight en des put out fer home."

I stopped, took a deep breath, and looked over at Katie. She had snuggled down under her blanket and was almost asleep.

"But why didn't Mr. Fox just eat the little rabbits?" she asked in a soft voice. "Why did he want the sugarcane and the water?"

"He had to find an excuse to eat them. He had to find them being disobedient. If they were bad, then he could punish them. So he told them things to do that he didn't think they could do."

"But why would a fox be afraid of a rabbit?"

"I don't know," I laughed. "It's just a story to keep young'uns quiet. Half the stories I told Samuel didn't make any more sense than that."

Katie closed her eyes and in a minute or two was breathing deeply. I slipped off her bed, turned the light down low, and went to my room.

So that's how we began reading and sharing stories with each other.

On most evenings Katie would maybe play something on the piano—sometimes she'd even sing, or we'd sing together. I taught her more of my songs, and she taught me some of hers. Then we'd go upstairs and get into our bedclothes and then would read or tell stories till we got sleepy. One of our favorites was *Pilgrim's Progress*. In between times she wanted me to tell her some of the slave stories I knew.

WORKING AND LEARNING TOGETHER

22

I WOKE UP ONE MORNING FEELING CHILLY. IT HAD BEEN a little stormy and I guess the weather had turned.

Shivering, I got up and went to Katie's room. She was gone.

I went downstairs and found her in the kitchen kneeling at the stove.

"The fire went out," she said, glancing up from the open door. "But I can't get it started."

I went over to take a look.

"Your chunks of wood are too big, Miss Katie. You can't start a fire without using tiny little bits of dry wood to get them going first. And you gotta have paper first, then you lay little pieces of kindling crossways on top of it, making a little pile. Let's go outside and get some kindling and I'll show you how."

Katie went out to the woodpile with me. We were about out of kindling, so I set a couple of chunks up on the chopping block to cut some more. Katie watched with I think as much awe to see me handle the ax as I had watching her play the piano. I reckon everybody's got different kinds of skills, though I didn't hardly think cutting wood or singing a revival song could compare with playing a minuet by somebody named Mozart.

"Would you show me how to do that, Mayme?" said Katie after I'd sent a few little thin slices splintering off the chunk.

"It can be dangerous, Miss Katie," I warned. "You gotta watch out for your fingers."

"But I've got to learn to do these things sometime," she said. "I helped my mama some, but I was never very good at it. I didn't like to work. But watching you makes me want to learn how. Look at my hands— they're all soft and smooth. I need to get them toughened up like yours."

"I think most white ladies *like* smooth hands, Miss Katie."

"Not me. My mama's hands were rough too after my daddy left for the war."

"Okay, then, but you gotta promise you'll keep your fingers out of the way of the blade."

"I promise."

I handed her the ax. "Take it in both your hands, and

start that way. Just bring the blade down about an inch from the edge."

She tried it but missed the chunk completely. The tip whacked into the chopping block with a thud and stuck. I yanked it out and handed it back to her.

"Try it again. The most important thing is to get a chunk of wood without knots and with nice straight grain. Then you can just splinter the kindling right off the edge."

She tried a few more times and got some pieces to slice off. Then we took what we'd cut into the house and I showed her about building the fire. Already Katie had the makings of a blister starting on her right palm.

It was while we were making the fire that I noticed how few phosphorous matches we had left. Katie had to use three or four before she could get one to light. I hadn't thought of it before. We'd be in a predicament once we started running out of things like that. I knew people had fire long before they invented matches. But I didn't know how to start one from nothing and didn't want to try.

After that we started banking up the fire every night to make sure we still had hot coals in the morning. For now there was plenty of firewood out by the barn, though I had to chop up new kindling every couple of days.

That night Katie read to me from a book named *Rollo in London* written by a man called Jacob Abbott. Rollo was traveling around the world with his uncle George. The next day she showed me a whole set of

Rollo books in her room.

"What country would you like to know about?" Katie asked me. "South America or Africa or Rome or Paris."

"I'm sorry, Miss Katie, but I've never heard of any of them," I said. "I'd never even heard of London before last night. But anything you want to read is fine by me."

"I am tired of Rollo anyway," said Katie. "So tonight I will read to you from *Goody Two-Shoes*. But it will not do for me to do all the reading. You should read too."

"But I don't read too great."

"Then you can practice by reading the McGuffey Readers," said Katie. "That's how I learned to read."

"Would you help me, Miss Katie?"

"I will go get the first one right now," she said, jumping up. "I know where they are on the bookshelf. I remember putting them away myself."

She returned in a minute holding a little brown book. She handed it to me.

"That's a funny-looking word," I said, pointing to the cover.

"*The Eclectic First Reader*," Katie read. "I don't know what *eclectic* means either," she said with a little laugh, "but, here, I'll find you something to read. I bet you can read just fine."

She turned the pages, looking at one lesson after another, then stopped.

"Here's one," she said. "I'll start. 'Come, let us go into thick shade,' " she began. " 'It is noonday, and the summer sun beats hot upon our heads. The shade is pleasant and cool. The branches meet above our heads and shut out the sun like a green curtain.' "

She stopped and pointed to where she was.

"Now you keep going, Mayme," she said, putting the book in front of me.

"Okay, I'll try," I said. " 'The . . . grass is . . . soft to . . . our feet,' " I began slowly, " 'and the clear—' "

I hesitated. "What's that next word?"

"Brook," said Katie.

" '—and the clear brook . . . washes . . . the r-r-oot . . . washes the roots of the trees.' "

"I knew you could do it," said Katie. "That was very good. Keep going, and I'll read along with you to make it easier."

" 'The cattle can lie down to sleep in the cool shade,' " we read out loud together, " 'but we can do better. We can raise our voices to heaven. We can praise the great God who made us.' "

As we read, Katie waited a moment to let me try each word alone, then said it to help me along. Pretty soon, as I got more comfortable with it, I felt like I was reading it myself even though she was saying it with me. She was a natural-born teacher.

We finished the little story together.

" 'He made the warm sun and the cool shade,' " we read, " 'the trees that grow upwards, and the brooks that run along. The plants and trees are made to give fruit to man. All that live get life from God. He made the poor man, as well as the rich man. He made the dark man, as well as the fair man. He made the fool, as well as the wise man. All that move on the land are His, and so all that fly in the air, and all that swim in the sea. The ox and the worm are both the work of His hand. In Him, they live and move. He it is that doth give food to all of them, and when He says the word, they all must die.' "

I couldn't help smiling when we set the book down.

"Thank you, Miss Katie," I said. "That was fun. It got easier with you helping me."

"And every little bit you read will make it easier and more fun," she said. "So let's go through the book, and you read every story and learn the words at the end. See, the next story is called 'The Lame Dog,'" she said. "You try to read it by yourself first a time or two, then when you are ready, we will read it together. We'll do a new one every morning and evening."

LATE ONE AFTERNOON I was milking the cows by myself. Katie must have been off doing something else. As I milked, without realizing it, I started squeezing in rhythm, humming a tune, and after a while I was singing softly to the time and the sound of the milk spraying out into the bucket.

Singing is what black folks do when they work. The men sang in the fields hoeing cotton and picking corn. Everybody, even the children, had to pick the corn when it was ripe, from sunup till sundown, and I remember the sounds of the singing clear as yesterday. The women sang when they washed the clothes. And us young'uns sang when we worked and played. Singing's just what black folks did. It made the work go by a heap easier.

As I was milking away, all at once I realized Katie had come up behind me. I looked around and stopped.

"What was that you were singing, Mayme?" she asked.

"A song we used to sing."

"Sing it again," she said, sitting down on another stool.

I started milking again, got the rhythm of my squeezing going like before, and then started singing along with it.

> "Hit's a gittin' mighty late, w'en de Guinny-hins
>   squall,
> En you better dance now, ef you gwineter dance
>   a tall.
> Fer by dis time ter-morrer night you can't hardly
>   crawl,
> Kaze you'll hatter take de hoe ag'in en likewise
>   de maul—
> Don't you hear dat bay colt a kickin' in his stall?
> Stop yo' humpin' up yo' sho'lders—Dat'll never
>   do!
> Hop light, ladies, Oh, Miss Loo!
> Hit takes a heap er scrougin', Fer ter git you
>   throo—
> Hop light, ladies, Oh, Miss Loo!"

I looked over at Katie, and she was smiling and tapping her foot.

"There's another verse," I told her.

"Oh, keep singing," she said. So I continued, then she joined me on, "Hop light, ladies, Oh, Miss Loo!" We laughed and laughed.

Katie got off the stool, then brought it over, sat down and started to milk the next cow. I watched her pull the pail underneath and just get to milking away. She didn't seem to mind a bit like she had that first day.

I WORKED ON my lessons like Katie had said, reading one new story every morning and another at night.

I'd work my own way through them slowly once, sounding out the words I didn't know, and then a second time. Katie would sit down with me, and we'd read it aloud together. Within just a few days of practicing, I was reading a lot better than before, though the stories got harder real quick. Sometimes I would do two in a day, sometimes three. I especially liked the one called "The Snow Dog and Boy."

Within about a week I was through with the stories in the first reader, and Katie excitedly brought me the next, called *The Eclectic Second Reader*. I saw right off that the printing was smaller. The book was thicker too.

"This looks harder," I said. I didn't see how I would ever get through it.

"Just try it," said Katie, looking at the first story, then turning the page. "Here, read Lesson Two." She handed me the book.

"I don't even know that first word," I said.

"It's 'James,' " said Katie.

"All right . . . 'James,' " I read, " 'it is now mor-mor

150

. . . ning. Morning. The sun is just peep . . . peeping over the hills in the east. Get up, my boy, for the sun has just . . . risen.' "

"There, you see," Katie smiled, "you can read it fine. Just keep going with one or two stories a day, and we'll keep reading them aloud together. You're doing real well, Mayme."

As I read more in the second reader, Katie was showing me some of her favorite books too, and I began to spend time in front of the bookshelf, pulling out volumes and looking at some of them myself. She told me about biographies of famous people written by Peter Parley—she especially liked the one about George Washington—and the silly book of funny drawings and verses called the *Book of Nonsense*. She was also real fond of some fairy tales by a man named Hans Christian Andersen.

"Sometimes those fairy tales come alive in my mind," she said, "when I'm at my secret place in the woods." Then she stopped and got a funny look on her face.

"What secret place?" I asked.

"I've never told anybody about it," she said slowly, "not even my mother. It's a place I found in the woods."

"Can I see it?" I asked. Katie promised to show it to me sometime soon.

23

I CAME UPSTAIRS WITH AN ARMLOAD OF CLEAN clothes from the line outside. Katie had insisted that I wear some of her mother's dresses. At first I wouldn't hear of it, but finally I realized the rags I was wearing were eventually going to fall right off me. So I made her pick out two of the plainest ones, and I had one to wear when I washed the other.

Anyway, I was carrying a load up the stairs and came upon Katie in her room, bent over her writing desk.

"What are you doing?" I asked from the doorway.

"Writing a poem."

"A poem . . . you really write poems?"

"Yes. This is my poem book. I haven't written one since . . . you know, before everything that happened."

"What does it say?" I put the clothes on the bed and sat down.

"It's a little embarrassing to let someone else read your poems," she said, her cheeks pink.

"Please show me, Miss Katie. I've never thought up a poem in my life."

"All right. But promise you won't laugh."

"I would never laugh, Miss Katie. If you thought of it all by yourself, that makes it special."

"Okay, then—here it is. It's called, 'Mama's Gone.'

"When morning comes, the voices of the birds
  still ring.
They think it's the same as before.
But I've got no song to sing.
I'm quiet, and cold to the core.
My music has turned to dismay.
Mama's gone away.

Outside my window, everything looks drab and
  odd.
There's nothing to do but cry.
What makes bad things happen, God?
Can you tell me why?
What once was joy is only gray.
Mama's gone away."

Tears came to my eyes. "That's beautiful, Miss Katie, even though it's sad," I said. "It's kinda like a song. I'm sorry about your mama, but I think your poem is real nice. I never knew anybody that could make something like that up out of their own head."

"You make up stories, Mayme. I've never made up a story. And black folks make up poems and turn them into songs."

"Yeah, I reckon. But that seems different than this. Will you read me another?"

"Yes, if you want. Here's one I wrote at my . . . well, you know, my special place in the woods."

I nodded.

"Sometimes when I used to go there, I'd think of poems. Here's what I wrote."

She turned a couple of pages, then took a breath and started to read.

"There's little Miss Rabbit, Mrs. Robin, and
grand big Mr. Deer.
They all come to drink.
They don't mind if I'm here,
because they know I'm their chum.

Mrs. Robin sings. Mr. Deer tiptoes through the
grass. Miss Rabbit scampers along.
But Mr. Raccoon is shy.
He doesn't think I belong
in this place where the animals come.

People and animals ought to be friends. We have
the same home. We share this earth.
There shouldn't be fear.
God gave all creatures birth,
so friends is what we ought to become."

"That's right fine, Miss Katie. What's that one called?"
"I don't know. I haven't given it a name yet."
"Do deer and rabbits really come and drink when you are there?"
"Yes. But I only saw Mr. Raccoon once, and he never came back. I'm sad that he's afraid of me. That's why I wrote the poem."
It made me want to see her secret place even more.

MRS. HAMMOND

24

M AYME . . . MAYME, THERE'S A WAGON COMING!"
shouted Katie, running from the house.

I was near the barn mixing up some grain and water
to make slop for the pigs to eat.

"How close?" I asked, dropping the bucket. We both
headed back to the house at a run.

"I heard it and saw the dust from the road toward
town," she panted. "It's just coming through the field
and will be here any minute."

"Who is it?"

"I couldn't see. It's from the wrong direction to be
Mr. Thurston again."

"I'll go inside," I told her. "You'll have to talk to
them again, like last time."

"But—"

"I don't know what you'll say, Miss Katie," I interrupted her. "You'll have to see who it is and what they
want."

I tore off my muddy boots and ran inside.

As I hurried upstairs, Katie stationed herself by the
front door. I could hear the clatter and jingling and
snorting of horses pulling a buckboard even before the
bedroom door slammed shut behind me. I crouched
down and peeked over the edge of the window.

It looked like a woman was driving a team of two horses. The three dogs were running and barking around the wagon. Even from up where I was hiding, the expression on her face made me a little nervous. She looked like the kind of woman who had a perpetual scowl on her face, the type of person who made a habit of butting into other people's business. I doubted she'd be inclined to let sleeping dogs lie, pardon the expression since the dogs sure weren't sleeping right then.

I heard Katie open the door and walk out onto the porch.

"Hello, Miss Kathleen," the woman said. "Where's your mama?"

"She's not here, Mrs. Hammond."

"Where is she?"

"She's . . . away, ma'am, uh, on business."

"What kind of business?"

I could hear suspicion in the lady's voice so thick you could've cut it.

"I'm not sure, Mrs. Hammond."

"Well . . . hmm—I guess it can't be helped," said the lady, climbing down from the buggy. "Call your dogs off," she said with some irritation. "I do declare—"

And I heard Katie calming down the three dogs and calling them away from the lady. I peeked over the windowsill again and almost chuckled to see them standing around Katie like they were protecting her.

"Might as well deliver your mail, then," she said, handing over a bundle.

"Yes, ma'am," said Katie, standing firmly in place

156

as she took the letters.

"It's been piling up at the post office," Mrs. Hammond said. "That's when I realized I hadn't seen your mama for longer than usual. The mail's been collecting since that day you came to pick it up and said your mama was busy with the slaves. Do you remember?"

"Yes, ma'am."

"I started wondering if something might be wrong, not seeing her in all this time. So I thought I would bring it out and find out for myself. Is there anything wrong, Kathleen?"

"Uh . . ." began Katie in a hesitant voice.

One of the dogs started growling in its throat, and Mrs. Hammond stepped backward as did I from my window.

"Why hasn't your mama been to town to collect her mail?" she asked, glaring down at the dog. "And aren't you even going to invite me inside for a glass of water?" Mrs. Hammond went on. "Gracious, child, where's your manners? What's wrong with you today?"

"I'm sorry, ma'am. You're welcome to a glass of water."

Mrs. Hammond was already on her way inside with or without an invitation. I tiptoed toward the door in case I could hear more of the conversation drifting up the stairway.

Katie had followed Mrs. Hammond into the kitchen.

"Where's Beulah?" I heard the woman ask.

"I don't know, ma'am," answered Katie.

A *humph* of dissatisfaction sounded. I heard the clacking of the kitchen pump followed by running water.

"Well, tell your mama to come and see me," Mrs. Hammond said after a short time. "I don't like the sound of her being so busy she can't even come to town to pick up her mail, especially when she hasn't made a payment on her account at the store for three months. You tell her I don't mind carrying her along when times get lean, but I've got a business to run too. And there's a note in that stack of mail from Mr. Taylor. When he heard I was coming out to Rosewood, he asked me to tell your mother that he wants to talk to her about her loan that's due in two months. Can you remember that, Kathleen?"

"Yes, ma'am," Katie said meekly.

"Well, I hope so."

She let out a sigh, then I heard footsteps moving toward the door. "Goodness, child, I thought you'd have grown up more by this time. You must be a grief to your poor mother sometimes."

The door shut.

I hurried back to the window and was relieved to see the buckboard disappearing along the road the way it had come.

The Secretary Again

25

WHEN I GOT DOWNSTAIRS, KATIE WAS STILL standing in the kitchen, not exactly trembling from the encounter, but almost.

I saw the mound of mail sitting on the kitchen table. Without thinking, I went over and absently started thumbing through the stack. There were some advertisements for farming equipment and seeds and that kind of thing, a magazine, a rolled-up newspaper, and two or three letters, and—

All of a sudden I realized what I was doing. I froze, then jerked my hand away.

Katie must have seen the motion and it brought her back to herself.

"What's wrong, Mayme?" she asked.

"Nothing, I was just forgetting myself, that's all," I said. "Sometimes I got to remind myself that this ain't my house. Not that I ever really forget, but you know what I mean, and I got no right to be prying into other folks' affairs. I'm sorry, Miss Katie."

"You've got as much right as me, Mayme. There's nobody here but you and me, so who else is going to look at the mail?"

She moved to the table and picked up the stack of papers and things. "I guess I'll go put this on

Mama's desk," she said.

I followed her upstairs. She glanced through the pieces like I had.

"Any of those things from anyone you know?" I said.

"I don't think so," she replied. "I don't recognize any of the names."

"Even those letters?"

She shook her head. "But you can look through them if you like," she said, handing me the letters.

"I don't know what I'd be looking for."

"Well, I'd like you to anyway, just in case," she said.

We got to the little office and went in.

"I want you to look through all of it," said Katie, pointing to the desk.

"But, Miss Katie, I can hardly read compared to you."

"But you might see something important."

"All right, if you want me to, but—"

"I do. You were right when you told me I should decide what to do," she said. "But I haven't. I'm afraid, Mayme. I don't want to go live with *any* of my uncles, and Mama says her sister in the North is mad at us. I don't know what to do, Mayme. I want to tell someone the truth, but . . ."

She began to cry.

"All right, Miss Katie," I said as comfortingly as I knew how. "I'll try to help you figure out what to do. But you sit here with me."

I sat down in the big desk chair and looked through the mail again more slowly this time. I saw a short note that was just a sheet of paper folded twice.

"Who's this Mr. Taylor?" I asked, looking at the signature.

"The man at the bank," Katie answered.

"What does this say?" I said, handing her the sheet.

"It says he wants to talk to my mama," she said, then read from the paper, " 'about the balance of one of the loans that's due in September to clear off the first lien against the plantation.' "

"What does that mean?" I asked.

"I don't know," said Katie, shaking her head. "I took some money to him for Mama once."

"Let's look at the letter from your uncle Ward again," I said. "Where did you put it?"

"I think it's in one of these cubbyholes . . . here it is," said Katie, pulling it out and unfolding it.

"Read it to me again," I said.

Katie repeated what she had read before, then kept going.

" 'I got to do something with it,' " she read. " 'There's men who think the way to git rich is taking from men who's done the work rather than finding it for theirselves. I broke my back for three years to git this, and I ain't gonna let them steal it now. Maybe you can help, Rosie. But I wouldn't do nothing to put you in no danger. I only might need a place to stash it for a spell.' "

"Who's Rosie?" I asked.

"My mama," Katie replied.

"Oh . . . all right, keep going," I said.

" 'I'm leaving California directly. It's getting too

crowded with newcomers and folks who'll do you in if you don't watch yourself. I got me plenty to last awhile, enough to make me a stake for a small spread someplace, if only I can git out of it alive and stay a few steps ahead of them.' "

"Who's he talking about?" I asked.

Katie shook her head.

"I don't know anything about it," she said. " 'So I'll be there directly, Rosie,' " Katie read. " 'Whatever you do, don't tell Templeton I'm coming. I got a feeling he'd be after what I got too if he found out.' "

"What does it mean?" I asked again.

"I don't know," said Katie.

"Did he ever come?"

"I never saw him if he did," she said.

"So you only know this uncle here, this Templeton," I said.

"I've seen my uncle Burchard a few times too," she said. "Like I told you, his farm is on the other side of Charlotte. But he doesn't like Daddy. Mama said once that Uncle Burchard thinks Rosewood ought to be his because he's older than Daddy."

"What did she mean?" I asked.

"I don't know," replied Katie.

26

I WOKE UP EARLIER THAN USUAL THE NEXT MORNING. It was barely getting light and was still real quiet, though I heard the roosters starting about their morning racket.

I don't know what made me wake up so early. But I knew Katie wouldn't be up for an hour or more and I couldn't go back to sleep.

I got dressed and went downstairs, checked the fire, and added a couple of fresh logs. It was even too early to milk the cows. I went out for my necessaries, then came back into the parlor. I wasn't really thinking much of anything when I found myself standing in front of the bookshelves. We didn't go into the parlor much. Katie said the curtains had to be drawn closed all the time, since some of the windows were still broken, as well as to keep the sun off the fine furniture.

I hadn't really paid much attention to the books here since the day we started cleaning things up and putting them all away. Most of the books we'd been reading from were on a shelf in Katie's room. But once in a while I saw her standing in front of this big bookshelf and looking at the books, like they were full of memories. It was not a feeling I'd ever had about a book. But I could tell Katie thought they were special just from the way she held them in her hands.

I had found myself starting to feel that way about the books we read together. Once you knew what was inside them, they seemed to hold secret treasures— their words and stories became friends. I'm sure a lot of these books in the parlor reminded Katie of her mama. She said her mama used to read to her a lot.

On this morning I found myself staring at the shelves like Katie did, and then my eyes fell on a great big book, bigger than any four or five books put together, lying flat on one of the lower shelves. I'd never noticed it before, not even when we'd been picking the books up off the floor. I reckon Katie must have put it there.

I tried to pull it out, but it was heavy. I had to use both hands to lift it. I carried it to the sofa and sat down with it in my lap and opened it. The words on the first page in fancy writing said *Holy Bible*.

I kept turning and came to several pages in the front with writing on them, names and dates. Then near the bottom in small writing I saw Katie's name—*Kathleen O'Bannon Clairborne,* with the date 1850.

It wasn't long before I realized this was a list of Katie's kin, with the dates of their births and deaths and marriages and everything. I saw some of the names Katie had told me about, Templeton and Ward and Nelda and Burchard. I can't remember if Katie had told me her mama and papa's names before this or not, but now I saw that their names were *Richard* and *Rosalind,* and that she'd had three brothers, *Joseph, Caleb,* and *Jason.*

I don't know why, but seeing all those names in that list suddenly made me sad—more sad than I had been since I had come there.

I couldn't help remembering that I had no family left at all, leastways that I knew about. But here was a whole list of people who were Katie's family—some of them dead and others far away.

Then I got real lonely, lonelier than I'd ever been in my life. I couldn't help myself, I just started to cry.

I was completely alone. I didn't have anybody else in the whole world who cared about me or that would take care of me.

I don't know why the thought hadn't come to me before, but all at once I realized that I was an *orphan!*

The word sounded horrible to think it, much less say out loud. I just sat there quietly crying for a long time.

Gradually I found myself looking down at the Bible still in my lap. I looked at the names again, blurry through my tears. And I was reminded of Katie's parents and what had happened to them. And then it dawned on me—Katie was an orphan too.

Then I cried all over again, this time for Katie.

Without really thinking what I was doing, I put the Bible down on the sofa and slowly walked back up the stairs. I went into Katie's room and went to the bed, took off my shoes, pulled back the blanket, and crawled in next to Katie.

The movement disturbed her and she woke up.

"What is it?" she said sleepily.

165

"It's all right, Miss Katie," I said. "It's nothing. I just got real sad that's all." I choked back some tears. "I wanted to be next to you. I hope you don't mind." My voice sounded all quavery.

"I'm sorry, Mayme," she said, moving to face me. "It's nice and warm in here."

She put her arms around me and pulled me tight.

"You're always taking care of me," she said. "So now we'll pretend I'm your mama for a change."

I snuggled up close to her. I felt better already. Pretty soon we both went back to sleep, lying there side by side.

AFTER WE GOT up later, I showed Katie the Bible and told her what I'd been thinking. We sat down close together for a long time with it between us looking through it, looking at the pictures of Bible scenes. Every once in a while Katie would read a verse or two out loud.

I sat thinking how good it would be to be able to read "the Good Book," as my mama used to call it, for myself. I would work real hard and practice with the stories in the McGuffey Readers like Katie suggested. We had already gone through four or five more stories. It was starting to get easier and I was beginning to recognize words more quickly.

As I sat there I also found myself remembering things from my life I hadn't thought of in a while, the sound of spirituals in the evening around the fire.

One of my favorites was "Steal Away." I could hear them singing it even now, slow and deep and with men finding harmonies down low, and women finding them up high.

Steal a-way, steal a-way . . . steal a-way to Jesus.
Steal a-way, steal a-way . . . steal a-way home.
I ain't got long to stay here.

It almost made me cry just to hear it in my mind.

I remembered the grown-ups talking about slavery and the children of Israel in Egypt. *"Ole Pharaoh,"* my grandpapa said, *"he treat de Israelites jist like de white folks treat us. But someday, we'll git outta our Egypt too. Don' know who our Moses'll be, but he'll come along by'n by."*

And then the song made it seem like we were the children of Israel ourselves.

Go down, Moses, way down in Egypt's land. Tell ole Pharaoh, Let my people go . . .

Once the songs started in my brain, I couldn't get them to stop.

Oh, freedom, oh, freedom, oh, freedom. An' befo' I'd be a slave, I'll be buried in my grave, an' go home to my Lord an' be free . . . sounded through my memory.

All night, all day, angels watching over me, my Lord . . .

Again my grandpapa's voice came back to me. This time I could hear him saying, *"Neber leave what der Good Book say, chil' . . ."* and, *"Whatever else you do, always make sho' you do what He tells you. . . ."*

Then my mama saying, *"You be a good girl, Mayme, chil'. Dat day's a comin' 'for long, a day I might not live to see. But you'll see it. You'll be a free black girl one day, Mayme, so you make me proud, little girl."*

And then the sound of singing again . . .

Gone are the days when my heart was young and gay.
Gone are my friends from the cotton fields away.
Gone from the earth to a better land I know.
I hear their gentle voices calling, Old Black Joe.

The slave life had been a hard life, I reckon, harder for grown-ups than for a girl like me. But it still had some good memories that were now gone forever. Whatever became of me, I'd never be with my family again. I'd likely end up with some other colored folks—maybe with a family someplace. They'd be family to each other.

But not me. I'd always be the orphan girl without a family of her own. I could almost hear *their* voices calling, not for old black Joe, but for the "orphan girl." That's probably what they'd call me too.

I cried to think of my mama, and her words kept haunting me . . . *"Be a good girl . . . a free black girl . . . make me proud."*

I came back to myself and Katie and me were still sitting beside each other, and Katie was still slowly thumbing through the pages, pausing occasionally to look at a picture or a verse.

Suddenly an idea came to me. Why hadn't I thought of it before?

My mama had had a Bible too, smaller one than this—nice, though it was real old. She always looked around like she didn't want anyone to see it or know that she had it when she pulled it out of its hiding place. I'd never thought about it, but maybe it wasn't ours, or maybe Mama thought someone would take it away. She read to us out of it every once in a while.

What if Mama's Bible had the names of my family in it? I thought.

Maybe I had kinfolk still alive too! I might not be able to find where they were. But if I could find out their names, that would be more than I knew now. And maybe I could find them someday.

"Miss Katie," I said excitedly. "I just remembered that my mama had a Bible too. I gotta go back to where we lived and see if I can find it."

"Can I go with you?" she asked.

Suddenly my wild idea didn't sound so good. What if we were seen? What if someone else came here while we were gone and found Rosewood empty?

Katie must have already thought the same thing.

"What if someone comes while we're gone?" she wondered.

"Maybe it's not too good an idea," I nodded. We sat quietly for a while, then I said, "But I gotta go. I gotta see if I can find the Bible and if I have any kin left. I want to know."

"Please let me go with you," Katie begged. "We'll just hope nobody comes while we're gone."

"I suppose we could get up real early and ride fast—"

"Yes, let's!" said Katie.

"All right," I said. "We'll go tomorrow."

RETURN

27

I DIDN'T SLEEP MUCH THAT NIGHT, AND I WAS UP before dawn. I had to wake Katie and she was pretty sleepy at first. But after we'd had a quick break-fast, she was wide-awake. The danger of it made it seem like an adventure, and we were both pretty keyed up—excited and scared at the same time.

Even though I hadn't been paying that much atten-tion when I'd wandered into Rosewood, as I'd thought about it since, I had some idea which way I'd come. I hadn't been but a few miles or so from my old planta-tion in the past, but somehow I was pretty sure I could find it. And when I told Katie that our master's name had been McSimmons, she said she remembered that name being associated with a family on the other side of Greens Crossing, she thought toward the east. That seemed to make sense to me. So that's the direction we headed.

We rode on two horses rather than hitching up a buggy, so we could go through fields and woods if we needed to. We went on the roads at first and rode as fast as we could manage. But once the sun was good and on its way into the sky, I led us off the roads and we stayed in woodsy areas where we wouldn't be seen.

I told Katie that sometimes one of our master's men would gather some of us young'uns in a wagon and take us off to collect wood. Looking around, I started seeing things I recognized. Not long after that I knew my way, and pretty soon I knew we were getting close to the McSimmons plantation and its colored town.

We came through a woods to the edge of a field, and I could see the house and other buildings I recognized. We watched carefully for a while but saw no signs of life. We dismounted and walked our horses across the field.

I had no idea what we would find. All kinds of strange feelings started surging through me as we approached. I got real scared, like those men might still be around, even though from the quiet I was pretty sure nobody was.

We walked up slowly past the big house in the distance and down the road to the slave quarters. Everything was just like I left it, except the bodies I hadn't been able to bury weren't there. I don't know what happened to them. Otherwise, it didn't look like a soul had been there since I'd left myself. The only sign that anybody'd ever lived there was the smell from the outhouses.

Katie looked around.

"You lived here?" she asked in a shocked tone. Clearly she had never seen such a place before, never even imagined that people would live in such a place.

Since the time I'd spent in her mama and daddy's house, it all looked a little different, a little worse, in my eyes too—the tumbled-down shacks, the dirt, the pitiful garden patches now all gone to weeds.

It's funny how things can look the same but different. It had only been—I didn't even know how long it had been . . . maybe a few weeks or a month. Katie and I had lost track of time. But as I stood there, it felt like a year—a lifetime—had passed. Everything I saw was from another time, almost like the person I remembered who had lived here, the girl I could picture in my mind, was somebody else and not me at all.

Having the two parts of me—the old and the new—looking at each other right then couldn't help but make me feel thoughtful and strange and sad.

I started to cry. Katie saw me and came over and put her arm around me. Just feeling her touch unleashed feelings I'd kept inside all this time.

I sobbed out loud. I couldn't help it. Maybe I suddenly realized that Katie was the only person I had in the whole world. And I didn't know how much longer I'd even have her.

I finally got myself calmed down. Slowly we started walking around. I remembered where I'd buried my ma and grandpapa and brothers and sisters, but I wasn't quite ready to see that yet.

I walked toward a little shanty.

"That's our house," I said.

Katie didn't reply.

I glanced over. Tears were spilling out of her eyes too, though quiet ones, not sobbing tears like mine had been. I moved toward the door. Katie hesitated. I reached out and took her hand. She followed me up the rickety steps, her hand tightly clutching mine. I couldn't tell if she was afraid or just feeling some of the same kinds of things I was.

I opened the door, and a scurrying sound startled us both. Katie jumped back and gave a little cry as we saw two or three rats running about. Katie grimaced but then slowly followed me the rest of the way inside.

Everything was just like I remembered it. It didn't look like a thing had been moved since that last day. Some food was still out on the table, all dried and spoiled now. It was ghostly quiet.

"Where was your room, Mayme?" Katie asked in a whisper.

"I didn't have a room, Miss Katie," I said. "All of us just slept in here."

The whole cabin wasn't much bigger than Katie's room. Several bunks stacked on top of each other against the wall, with their thin, dirty mattresses of straw, all looked the same.

"How . . . how many of you lived here?" Katie asked.

I had to stop a minute to think.

"Seven, I reckon," I said. "That was after my pa died. It would have been eight before that when the baby was born."

As I looked around, for the first time the thought came if there was anything I wanted from here. I'd left in such a hurry I hadn't had the chance to think about it before.

I looked at my few old clothes, folded on the end of a bunk. They seemed like rags now compared to the work dresses of Katie's mama that I was using.

"What's this?" Katie asked, walking toward my sleeping spot.

The sight brought new tears to my eyes.

"That's my crinkly rabbit," I said. "My mama made him for me. I call him Mister Krinkle."

She picked him up and handed him to me. He was old and dirty and nearly falling apart. The sight and feel of him filled me with pain.

"My mama knitted him for my fifth birthday," I said. "Then she filled him up with old rags and bits of straw."

"I like him," said Katie. "Let's take him home with us."

I sniffed and nodded.

Seeing the bed made brought another memory. I pulled back the mattress. Underneath were the pages of my diary.

I smiled. I'd almost forgotten them. They sure didn't look like much now.

I reached down and picked them up.

"What's that?" Katie wanted to know.

"Some things I wrote," I mumbled. I really didn't want to talk about it, at least not yet.

I laid the mattress back down, then remembered why we had come in the first place—the Bible.

There was a chest under Mama's bed where she'd kept her few clothes and things for the baby. I got down on my knees and dragged it out and pulled the top up. It was about half full of clothes and a couple of ragged blankets. I rummaged through down to the bottom, and sure enough, there it was. I took the Bible out, then stood up and showed it to Katie.

"It was my mama's," I explained again. "I don't think I've seen it in a while. I wasn't sure it would still be here, but here it is."

Seeing the Bible reminded me of the pretty blue pin of Mama's with the letters on it. She said they were the memories of her teardrops, and that always made her look at me with a sad smile. It ought to have been with my mama's other special things in the chest under the bed, but I looked carefully again, and there was no sign of it.

I stuffed my writing pages inside the Bible. We went back outside, Katie carrying Mister Krinkle and me carrying the old black Bible. I took a deep breath and walked in the direction of the graves, and then just stood looking down at the mounds of dirt I'd made over the bodies of my family.

"Is . . . is this—" Katie began.

"It's my mama and brothers and sisters and grand-papa," I said. "I buried them before I left."

A Lot of Growing Up to Do

28

T HE RIDE BACK TO ROSEWOOD AND THE REST OF THE day were quiet for both of us. Katie was sad for me and for what she'd seen. And maybe the finality of it was hitting me all over again.

That evening, I don't know what put it into my head but I felt like taking a bath. The idea of getting clean and fresh probably seemed like washing the past off me or something. I was still downcast about what I'd seen, and I reckoned maybe a bath would help.

"Miss Katie," I said after we had eaten supper, "would you mind if I took a bath in the tub upstairs?"

"Of course not, Mayme," she said. "Would you like me to help with the water?"

"That's right kind of you, but I can do it myself if—"

"I want to help," said Katie. "You always carry the water for me."

"That's different," I said. "I'm colored."

"It's not different now," said Katie.

We heated up the water in the kitchen and carried it up to the tub. We had to make a lot of trips up and down the stairs.

"My daddy said he was going to put pipes up here," Katie said, "so we could pump water up to the tub."

"That'd be rip-staver!" I said. "Imagine it—water in the house . . . and upstairs to boot!"

"I'll bring up the rest, Mayme," Katie added. "You can start your bath. Then I'll pour it over your back and head if you want to wash your hair. It'll feel good."

"Thank you, Miss Katie," I said.

I was taking a terrible liberty doing what I was doing. I usually washed in the creek or in the tub out by the barn. But I could tell it was all right with Katie, so I went ahead.

We hadn't ever undressed in front of each other. I suppose we were both a little embarrassed, not only about the difference in our skin, but how we'd been filling out recently like girls do. I hadn't as much as Katie, since I was taller and skinnier. But the changes in my body still took a little getting used to.

I got undressed and got into the tub of water while Katie was downstairs. I lay down in it and tried to forget that I was black, that I had no family left, that I really didn't belong anywhere. I closed my eyes and said to myself that it was all right just to enjoy this bath and that it was time I forgot the past.

Pretty soon I heard Katie coming back up the stairs lugging another pail of water. I sat up and wrapped my arms around myself.

She came in and put down the pot. "That was heavy," she said. "But I think it's just right, Mayme. If you want to soap up your head, I'll scoop it out in the cup and pour it over—"

She stopped and gave a little cry. "Mayme, what's

that?" she exclaimed. "What are those marks on your back?"

At first I didn't know what she was talking about. I reached up with one hand and tried to feel the top of my back. Then I remembered.

"Oh, that's nothing, Miss Katie," I said. "It's just from whippin's, that's all."

"Whippings—who whipped you!" she said, shocked at the very idea.

"The master, or the master's son or his men. Mostly the overseer. You should see some of the men. They got 'em all over. Mine's nothing. You should see the men that got cathauled."

"What's . . . what's that?" she asked.

"When the overseer ties a man face down to the ground, then takes a great big tomcat by the tail and hauls it along the man's back, while the clawing, screeching cat's trying to get loose and digging into the skin."

"Stop, Mayme! I can't stand it!" she cried, clasping her hands to her ears.

"All slaves've got flogging lines like this on their backs, Miss Katie, one way or another."

"Not . . . not my . . . not *my* daddy's slaves," she said in a faltering voice.

"Weren't no different here, Miss Katie," I said. "Slaves were slaves. Your daddy had whips and tomcats just like our master. I saw the whips in the barn. And I allow that he and his men knew how to use 'em too."

Katie crumpled to the floor and just sat there. She

didn't say anything for a spell. What was going on inside her I could hardly imagine. She was having to get used to a lot of new things these days.

"Mathias had a girl," she said after a bit in a real soft voice. "She was . . . she was about my age, just like you. I don't know what happened to her. I guess she's gone somewhere by now. I wonder if she had any . . . any whipping marks like you." Her voice dropped at the end like she could hardly bring herself to say the words.

I didn't answer. I didn't figure there was anything more to say.

I sat there in the bath, and Katie sat there on the floor, and neither of us said a word. Maybe it was finally dawning on Katie just how different we were, and how different were the worlds we'd come from.

"Oh, Mayme!" she said in a forlorn voice after a while, starting to cry. "What are we going to do?"

I don't know what put it in my head to say what I did, but this is what I answered her.

"We both got a lot of growing up to do, Miss Katie," I said. "And I don't reckon we got a lot of time to do it."

Then I remembered why I'd wanted to take a bath in the first place, to *forget* the past.

If I didn't get this bath started, the water was gonna get cold. So I started soaping.

"I'm ready for you to start pouring, Miss Katie," I said.

I didn't hear anything for a few seconds. But what I felt next wasn't the warm water falling over my head, but the warmth of Katie's fingers on my back, gently touching my scars.

"I'm so sorry, Mayme," she said. "I . . . I just didn't know."

MESSAGE IN THE BIBLE

29

F OR THE SECOND NIGHT IN A ROW I COULDN'T SLEEP very well. My mind was too full of thoughts and feelings and memories from having gone back to my old home, from the bath and from what Katie and I had talked about. I didn't know what to make of it all.

I had Mama's Bible snuggled in bed beside me, along with Mister Krinkle. I felt like a little girl again. Sometimes a body doesn't want to have to grow up, and right then I didn't.

I was lonely. I don't mind admitting it. Katie's poem about being alone without her mama stuck with me. I knew I could never make up for her mama any more than she could make up for mine. I was mighty glad to have Katie around. But I was still lonely. The stuffed rabbit and the Bible reminded me of Mama and kept me awake and then helped me to sleep.

I woke up thinking I heard a noise outside. But when I listened real close, there wasn't anything more.

Must have been the cows, I thought.

After I lay there awhile, I got up and carried Mama's Bible, which I reckon was my own now, down to the parlor. It was the only thing I could call my own in the whole world. Well, maybe except for Mister Krinkle. When I opened the book, there were the pages of my writing, which I had called my diary. It hardly looked like much now. I didn't think I wanted to look at them yet. I wasn't ready. I took the sheets back upstairs and put them in a drawer under some of the clothes Katie had given me to wear.

When I sat down again with the Bible, I looked for names like in the big Bible of Katie's. There were only a few—my grandmama's and grandpapa's, *Elijah and Faith Jukes,* then my mama's and daddy's, *Henry and Lemuela Jukes,* then all us kids, *Mary Ann, Samuel, Rachel, Robert,* and *Thelma.*

I turned to where the book was the most worn, toward the back, and tried to read some. But I couldn't make nothing of it. I guess I needed more practice in the reader before I could understand the sentences.

Just holding the Bible put me in a mind to think about God, and I realized I hadn't been thinking about Him at all. I hadn't asked for His help even once since all this had happened.

I'd never really prayed before that I could remember, personally I mean, with just God and me around. We'd always sung about God a lot, but I didn't remember praying except for praying the Lord's Prayer like I'd done when burying our dead families. My mama didn't talk much about God or praying, not like Grandmama and Grandpapa. Maybe religion was something mostly old folks did. I didn't know.

But even if that was so, I figured it didn't matter. Maybe I ought to get a start on it while I was still young. I reckon I needed all the help I could get, and I didn't mind admitting that any more than I minded admitting I was lonely.

So as I sat there I tried praying a little. I guess it was praying, though I'd never really heard people praying like what I was doing. The only praying I'd ever heard was at mealtime or when all the slaves from McSimmons's colored town would get together sometimes and sing. One of the men would stand up and talk or pray real loud, or when we went to the revival camps like I had told Katie about. But just a person all by themselves like I was, I didn't know if that's the way you were supposed to pray or not. But I figured it couldn't do no harm.

So I just started talking to God. In my mind, I mean, not out loud.

God, if you can help me and Katie outta this fix we're in, I said, *we'd sure appreciate it. I don't know what color you are, but I reckon you must be for black folks as well as white folks 'cause I know everybody prays to you. So I'm asking you to help this one black girl and this one white girl. I don't know what to do, and if you got any suggestions, maybe you could show us, however it is you do that.*

I looked at the Bible again, still in my lap. Just from

its limp black cover, I could tell it was old. I knew my mama could read 'cause she taught me the letters. I wondered if she had written in the names.

Holding the Bible filled me with memories of riding out in the back of a wagon to a camp meeting in the fields next to the white folks' tent, and then all the preaching and singing. As a little girl I hadn't understood anything of what was going on. For me it was just a chance not to work so hard for a spell and have fun. I hardly even knew what they meant when they talked and sang about God and salvation and Satan and redemption and Beulah land and all the rest. But now that I was alone in the world, I wanted to know for myself. God was about all I had left, along with Katie and my memories.

Again I found myself thinking back, and like it often did, music came into my mind.

Oh, de worril is roun' en de worril is wide—
Lord! 'member deze chillun in de mornin'—
Hit's a mighty long ways up de mountainside,
En dey ain't no place fer dem sinners fer ter hide,
En dey ain't no place whar sin kin abide.
W'en de Lord shill come in de mornin',
Look up en look aroun',
Fling yo' burden on de groun'.
Hit's a gittin' mighty close on ter mornin'!
Smoove away sin's frown—
Retch up en git de crown,
W'at de Lord will fetch in de mornin'!

I sat there with the Bible in my lap, slowly rocking back and forth. Then I started singing the rest of the camp-meeting song in my mind.

De han' er ridem'shun, hit's hilt out ter you,
Lord! 'member dem sinners in de mornin'!
De sperrit may be puny en de flesh may be proud,
But you better cut loose fum de scoffin' crowd,
En jine dese Christuns w'at's a cryin' loud
Fer de Lord fer ter comin' in de mornin'!
Shout loud en shout long,
Let de ekkoes ans'er strong.
W'en de sun rises up in de mornin'!
Oh, you allers will be wrong
Twel you choose ter belong
Ter de Marster w'ats a comin' in de morning!

I opened the Bible again. Inside the front was some real nice writing that wasn't made by any colored hand, that much I knew for sure.

To Lemuela Hawley, with love, Patience, whispered the words out of the past.

That must explain how my mama had come by this Bible, though I couldn't altogether make sense of the words. How much of it she'd read, I didn't know. But somebody'd read it, that much was for certain because there were markings and verses underlined.

I couldn't figure why my mama would have kept the Bible hidden. Maybe she was afraid the master would take it away.

Whatever the Bible's history, it had come to me

now. So I intended to make the best use of it I could. I really didn't know very much about what a Bible was. I just knew it was something "holy" and was a book about God and Jesus.

But I decided right then and there that I would put my mind to learning to read, if for no other reason than so I could read this Bible and find out what it had to teach me. Maybe that was the kind of help God could give me, like I'd prayed for. Maybe there was something in the pages of this book to help me. I didn't know for sure, but I thought I could figure it out. It seemed likely that God would want people to figure out about Him, so why shouldn't I?

Absently I turned through the first pages, before the actual book got started. On one of the blank pages, in the same nice handwriting that must have belonged to whoever had given Mama the Bible, was written: *Behold, I stand at the door, and knock: if any man hear my voice, and open the door, I will come in to him, and will sup with him, and he with me.*

It took me about a minute to read it. I couldn't exactly tell what it meant, what the door was, and why it was so important that the lady had written it in the front of this Bible. Below it was written *Revelation 3:20*. I knew that's how Bible verses looked, so I looked through the Bible and after a while, at the very end, found the word *Revelation* up at the top of the pages. Before too much longer I found the place marked 3:20, and there were the same words exactly like the ones written in the front of the Bible.

It was the first time I'd ever found anything in a Bible, and I couldn't help being a little proud of myself.

I read the words over again. I figured it was God talking to somebody.

I thought maybe I should read the rest of what the lady had written in front. I turned back, and beneath the first verse I had read I now saw, *Jesus is the door to eternal life (John 10:9). Open the door of your heart and let Him live there.*

I looked through the Bible again and pretty soon found the book called "John," just like I had the other book. Then I found the place marked 10:9.

This isn't so hard! I thought.

"I am the door," I read, and I was glad the next words were all easy and pretty short, although I did have a little trouble with the last word of the verse. *"By me if any man enter in, he shall be saved, and shall go in and out, and find pasture."*

I didn't know all of what this meant either, but I was starting to get an idea that there was some kind of message here.

I read over the handwritten words again another time or two, then sat thinking for a spell. I didn't know what *sup with him* meant, but probably something about eating. I figured if there was such a thing as a door to my heart, and if it was a place that God could come to live, then it was sure a door that you oughta open so He could.

I still wasn't sure what the difference between God and Jesus was. People talked about them like they

186

were the same. I kind of figured *Jesus* must be God's actual name or something like that. But maybe it didn't matter so much even if they were different. Maybe if I opened my heart, both of them would come in at the same time.

So when I started praying again, I tried to do what had been written to my mama, as best as I knew how.

God, I prayed, or Jesus, if you're the same, I want to be a good girl. I'm all alone in the world now, so I figure I need your help just to get by. I'd like to open the door of my heart to you and have you live with me if you would. I don't know if I'll know it when you do. Maybe I'll still feel alone. But it'll be a big help and a comfort to me just knowing that you're with me and that you're taking care of me. Help me to be good, like my mama said. And like I asked before, if you got any suggestions about what we're supposed to do now that our kin are all gone, Katie and me would sure appreciate knowing it.

SERIOUS TALK

30

THAT VISIT TO MY LITTLE OLD HOUSE AND THE memories about my family got me thinking hard again about the future. There were those uncles of Katie's that I'd think about every once in a while, and it would make me a little jittery. Katie still hadn't done or said anything about what she planned to do, and I sure was uncertain about what was going to happen to me. I knew it was only a matter of time before I was discovered, and then I'd be in a nasty fix. It seemed to me Katie had to decide how she was going to get in touch with one or more of her kin.

Since we had only half a loaf left, one morning we were in the kitchen making bread, and I figured it was as good a time as any to talk to Katie about it again.

"You know, Miss Katie," I said, keeping my tone as matter-of-fact as I could, "sooner or later I gotta be moving on."

"Why, Mayme?" she said in the little-girl voice from the way she used to talk when I first came. Hearing it reminded me how much she'd changed already.

"Miss Katie," I began again as Katie pounded on the dough, "this ain't my place. You know that as well as I do. I'm a slave, you're white. I've been saying that you gotta find out about your uncles, or maybe that aunt of yours up North, whether she liked your mama or not. You're gonna have to get in touch with one of them by and by."

"But I don't want to," she replied.

"I don't see how it can be helped. And when that time comes, I'm gonna have to be gone."

"But why, Mayme? Why can't they let you stay with me?"

"If they found me here living in a white man's house, eating a white man's food, sleeping in a white man's bed, and wearing your mama's clothes like you're letting me do, they'd lynch me up or just kill me on the spot. Nobody's going to feel like making any allowances for me."

"But my mama and daddy are dead."

"What's that got to do with it?" I asked.

"Doesn't that make this my house?" she argued. "Why can't I just stay here with you? I don't want to go to my uncles. To my aunt. Not *anyplace* but here."

Every once in a while Katie would surprise me with some statement that showed down inside she was thinking about things too.

"I don't know, Miss Katie," I said. "You're just a girl. You just turned fifteen. They ain't gonna just let you stay here by yourself. Even less with me. Likely as not this whole place belongs to one of them now anyway, probably that brother of your daddy's you were telling me about who you said wanted it. I think there's some way things are given to other people when folks die. Whose family's was this plantation? Your mama's or your daddy's?"

"I don't know."

"Must be your daddy's kin if your mama's from up North. No matter. None of that answers the problem of my being here or what's gonna happen to you. You gotta work on what you're gonna do, Miss Katie."

"Why can't you just be *my* slave?" she asked, looking at me with those big innocent eyes. The question took me so off guard I didn't know what to say.

"You can be my own personal slave," she repeated.

"It ain't as simple as that," I said finally. "You're just a girl. You can't own a big place like this and have a slave of your own. Your kinfolk are gonna want to get their hands on it. I don't mind staying and helping you for a spell. But someday somebody's gonna come and find us here, and then I'll get into bad trouble sure as I'm colored and you're white."

"Who's going to get you in trouble?" asked Katie.

"Anyone who finds me here. That Mr. Thurston fella, or that busybody lady from town. Or one or more of your kin. All white folks don't take as kindly to coloreds as you, Miss Katie. You've been real kind to me. But don't you know there's white folks who'd want to hang me from a tree till I was dead just for coming into a white man's house or touching his daughter?" I thought I might as well say it straight out.

Katie's hands went still in the dough. She had no idea what things were really like.

"Don't you understand, Miss Katie, I'll be in real bad danger if anybody sees me here. And you might be too, if the wrong people find you here, or if those men who killed our families came back. That thing I was telling you about before called rape that you don't need to know about, it sometimes happens when bad people find pretty girls like you alone, and it's real bad, Miss Katie."

"But nice people like Mr. Thurston and Mrs. Hammond and Henry at the livery stable, they wouldn't hurt me."

"Then they'd still take you away—and send *me* away."

"But I'll tell them you're my slave. I'll tell them you're my *friend*."

The word stunned me as much as my talking about being hung had stunned Katie. I just stood staring back, not sure I'd heard her right.

How could a white girl and a colored girl be *friends?*

I almost started to cry.

I tried to smile. "That's right kind of you to say, Miss Katie," I said after a minute. I couldn't look her in the eye right away. I thought I'd either start crying or else throw my arms around her.

"But I still don't think folks'd listen," I finally said, trying to keep her paying attention to the facts. "It might make 'em even more determined to see me swinging from a tree. And you could get in a heap of trouble yourself. White folks in the South have got a word for white people they hate near as much as coloreds—"

I paused a minute, not quite sure I should say it. "Well, it's nigger lover," I finally said. "You don't want folks calling you that, Miss Katie."

It was quiet for a while.

"Don't you see, Miss Katie," I went on after a bit, "all I'm trying to do is find a way for us to protect you, and if that means you getting in touch with some grown-up to help you so that no harm comes to you, then maybe that's what we gotta do. That Mrs. Hammond, though I ain't sure I like her much, sounds like she could help you find your kin."

"I don't want to find my kin."

"You got to."

"But what will happen to *you,* Mayme?"

"I don't know, Miss Katie. But I'm a little older than you, so I reckon I can take care of myself. I'll probably find some other coloreds and ask them to help me. I'll be all right. No black folks would turn out one of their kind who's in trouble. It's what will happen to *you* that we gotta think about first."

"Why, Mayme? Why do we have to think just about me?"

" 'Cause this is your home and you're white. I don't belong here anyway."

"You belong here now, Mayme."

"That's nice of you, Miss Katie," I said. "But we still gotta figure out what to do so you don't get into a fix worse than you're in now."

Katie was quiet. I didn't know yet if she really understood what I had been trying to get across to her.

She turned and went upstairs to her room. I could hear her crying. I didn't go up myself, though. What else could I say? I had been trying to get her to face what her situation really was like.

And mine too. I felt bad for her, but I didn't know what else to do. I was pretty sure I was doing the right thing by making her think about the future, even if she didn't want to. The next person to come along might not be as harmless as Mrs. Hammond or Mr. Thurston had been.

When they were ready, I put the loaves of bread in the oven to bake.

KATIE'S SPECIAL PLACE

31

THE BREAD WAS COOLING ON THE TABLE WHEN KATIE came back down a little while later.

She wandered outside. From the window I watched her walk down the road in the opposite direction from town, then turn and go across a field. I didn't know where she was going but thought I ought to keep track of her. So I followed, keeping a ways behind, though I didn't try to keep out of sight.

She walked through two or three fields, then disappeared into the woods beyond. One of the dogs had come along too, and once he went barking into the woods like he was chasing something or someone. But I couldn't see anything myself. Must have been a rabbit.

I ran to try to catch up and barely saw Katie through

the trees ahead. Then she disappeared again. I hurried on, squeezing through trees and brush. I'm sure I sounded like a herd of cows crashing around. Then suddenly I came into a pretty little green clearing.

There was Katie in the middle of it, sitting across the grass on a rock next to a little pond with a creek running in and out of it.

She turned her head toward me. I could tell she had been crying.

"This is beautiful, Miss Katie," I said softly.

"It's my special place in the woods," she said with a sad smile. "It's always been a secret up till now, but I don't mind you being here. I come here to talk to the animals and write poems. I haven't been here since . . . since before . . ."

I walked over and sat down on the grass beside the rock. The dog seemed to know he shouldn't keep racing around in this peaceful place and settled down beside me.

"I'm sorry, Miss Katie," I said. "I didn't mean to upset you back there with what I said. I'm just worried about you."

"I know," she said, her voice so low I could barely hear the words. "You're just trying to help me, Mayme. But I just don't know what to do. It's all so awful . . . I wish I could have my mama back!" She began to cry again.

I reached out and took her hand. She gripped it tight. Pretty soon I was crying too. I don't know if it was for Katie or for me—most likely both of us.

We sat awhile like that, just crying and sniffling.

"You know, Miss Katie," I finally said, "a few days ago I did something I'd never done before."

"What's that?"

"I talked to God a little. I asked Him if he could help us."

"You mean you prayed."

"I reckon that's what I did."

"I pray every night like my mama taught me. But I'm still sad. It doesn't seem to help."

"I found some verses in my mama's Bible that were about opening the door of your heart so Jesus could come in. I did that. I can't say for sure that He walked in, but I think so."

"What happened after you asked Him?" asked Katie, sounding now more curious than anything.

"Nothing," I said. "At least I didn't *feel* different. But I guess I got the impression that God's gonna take care of us somehow."

"Would you tell me what to do, Mayme? I want to ask Him that too."

"I don't know, Miss Katie . . . one of the verses said that Jesus is the door, and the other one said that God is knocking on the door and that if you open it, He'll come in. It's the door to our hearts, I reckon."

"How do you open the door?"

"I don't know . . . maybe ask Him to turn the handle and come in, I guess. That's all I did. In the front of the Bible it said you should open the door of your heart and let Him live there. So I just told God that I wanted Him to come into my heart."

"Then I will too," said Katie firmly. She let go of my

hand and folded hers in her lap, then bowed her head and closed her eyes. "God," she said out loud. "I'm all alone and don't know what to do, like Mayme has been telling me. So I want to open the door of my heart to you too, and ask you to help me. Please come in and show me what you want us to do. And thank you, God, for bringing Mayme here. She's about the best friend I could ever imagine. Amen."

I started crying again. Nobody'd ever said something so nice about me before, and certainly not to God.

"Thank you, Miss Katie," I said through my tears. "Did you really mean that?"

"Of course I meant it, Mayme. I don't know what I would do without you. I'd probably be dead by now."

"No you wouldn't!" I laughed as I sniffed again. "You'd have managed to take care of yourself."

"I don't know how. Anyway, it doesn't matter. I believe God sent you to help me, and I'm glad."

We sat for a long spell just looking at the water and listening to the creek.

"Are you going to write a poem about today?" I asked after a bit.

"I was just thinking about that," replied Katie. "I think I will. It will be about God and the friend He sent me."

I couldn't help but smile at the thought of me, Mary Ann Jukes, being in a poem!

"I reckon we oughta be getting back, huh?" I said.

We both stood up. Katie turned toward me, then

reached out and gave me a big hug. We stood like that for probably a whole minute, neither of us giving thought about one of us being white and the other being black. Then the dog started sniffing around us and whimpering like he wanted to get in on the act. We laughed and started back.

I reckon I realized it myself now too . . . we were just *friends*.

QUESTIONS

32

A S WE WERE WALKING BACK, I SAID, "YOU KNOW, Miss Katie, I've been thinking about that letter from your uncle. Are you sure you don't know what he was talking about, or remember him coming for a visit or anything?"

"I don't think so. But now that you remind me . . . maybe I do remember hearing Mama and Daddy talking about him once, a while ago. I wonder if he visited and they were talking about him afterwards."

"Could that have had something to do with why your other uncle came for the visit a year ago?" I asked.

"Maybe so," she said thoughtfully. "Now that you mention it, he asked a lot of questions."

"I bet your uncle—what was the name of the one

who was in California?"

"Uncle Ward."

"I bet he found gold in California. I heard tell of California having lots of gold. A slave ran away once and everyone said he was going to California to find gold. So if your uncle found some, maybe your other uncle wanted it."

"Uncle Templeton didn't say anything about any gold, although he did ask if Mama had heard from Uncle Ward."

"What about—"

All of a sudden I just had an amazing thought. "Could he have brought it *here,* Miss Katie?" I asked.

"Brought what here?"

"The gold he found in California. Could he have had it with him when he came?"

"I don't know. But what would—"

"Don't you see what I mean! What if he never came back for it?"

"Do you mean—you mean it might still be here . . . *now?*"

"Yes," I replied. I couldn't help but be excited. "Could it *still* be here?"

"I . . . I'm not sure," said Katie, "but it could be—"

"That letter made it sound like he was afraid and wanted your ma to help. What if he gave it to your mama to keep for him, but then maybe he got killed in the war so he never came back. And if he didn't—"

I stopped when Katie's eyes got real big.

"What is it?" I said.

"I just remembered something! I remember hearing

Caleb and Joseph talking one day about Uncle Ward!"

"What did they say?"

"I wasn't paying much attention. But now that I think about it, I remember hearing my mama and papa talking too, before my daddy left. Something about Mama keeping something for her brother, and then about him coming back, and giving it to him—"

"Just like I thought!" I exclaimed.

"But my daddy said he didn't think he would come back with a war on. Then they were talking about her brothers, Ward and Templeton, hating each other and what would happen if Uncle Templeton found out."

"If he didn't ever come back, then—" I said, "then it *could* still be here!"

We were walking pretty fast by now, our legs trying to keep up with our tongues.

"Is that what those bad men were after?" Katie asked, panting to keep up with my longer legs.

"Hmm . . . doesn't seem likely." I shook my head. "Otherwise why would they have killed your family and other folks around? Why would they have killed your ma if she was the one who knew where it was? Why wouldn't they have searched the place? Just doesn't seem likely to me."

We were both quiet for a while.

"Where might it be?" I wondered out loud. "Think, Miss Katie. Is there any place where your ma and pa might have hid something valuable? Did they have someplace like my mama's chest under the bed where they kept treasures, a box or a—what's that kind of thing called where people put stuff and lock it?"

"A safe? I think my daddy had one in his office."

"Show me."

We were pretty excited by the time we got back to the house. We hurried into the house and upstairs to the office.

Katie looked around, then walked to a picture on the wall and swung it open. It was attached on the side instead of the top. Behind it in the wall there was a black metal door with a round knob on it with numbers all around in a circle.

"There it is!"

"Can you open it?" I asked.

She tried the handle, but it was locked.

"That's gotta be where it is," I said. "How do you open it?"

Katie shook her head. "I think it's something like a puzzle. You have to turn the dial back and forth. I saw Mama fiddling with it once."

"But you don't know how to do it?"

She shook her head again.

"Maybe there's something in the desk that tells about it," I said, walking over and looking at the papers and boxes and files on top of it. "You gotta look, Miss Katie, and see if you can find something that tells about it."

"I will, Mayme."

"Maybe it better wait till later," I said. "I can smell that fresh bread down in the kitchen, and it's making me hungry."

"You're always hungry, Mayme," Katie laughed. "Let's go eat."

"Maybe we should finish the old half loaf first," I said. "And besides, the new ones will be too hot to cut."

UNEXPECTED VISITORS

33

N OW WHERE IS IT?" I SAID AS WE WALKED INTO THE kitchen.

Katie glanced around too, but the leftover half loaf of bread was nowhere to be seen.

"That's a mite odd," I said. "Did that dog follow us into the house when we came back from the woods?"

Katie laughed. "I've never seen him eat bread, and he sure isn't here now."

I shrugged and headed out to the barn while Katie worked on our lunch. I had to clean out the stalls after the morning's milking.

As I came in, something scurried into a dark corner. *Probably a barn cat,* I thought when I didn't see or hear anything more. *Maybe it's the critter that ate that missing bread,* I joked to myself as I climbed up into the hayloft to throw down some clean hay for the animals. I tossed down the bales, then clambered back down the notched pole to the barn floor.

I had just started to shovel the manure out of the stalls when suddenly Katie ran in, a look of terror on her face. Her eyes were huge, and she was trying to say something.

"There's . . . it's some . . . there's men coming. On horseback," she stammered.

A shiver went all through me. It was just what I'd been afraid of. After the two earlier visitors we'd had, and my talks with Katie about what was to become of us, I'd hoped the next people we'd encounter would be someone Katie trusted, someone who could help her—a relative or a friend, or maybe someone from nearby like a sheriff or a minister or something, or maybe even that Mr. Thurston fellow again.

But the first thing to come into my mind, when I heard her say *some men* was that marauding gang that had killed my family and hers. If they'd come back, I knew well enough what they'd do if they found us alone. They'd kill me and do things to Katie I didn't even want to think about. She was pretty enough and growing up. That much was plain to anyone who took a good look at her. And if they found an empty house, they might just decide to stay and take it over themselves.

I didn't need to tell Katie to be quiet. She was trembling from head to foot. It wasn't but a few seconds after she came in before I heard horses outside, then men's voices.

I set the pitchfork down as quietly as I could and crept to the door of the barn. I peeked out and saw a couple of men on horseback. Luckily it wasn't anything like the big band of riders from before. They were riding into the open space between the barn and the house.

I jerked my head back and scurried to Katie, grabbing her hand and motioning with a finger to my lips. I pulled her to a dark corner where we ducked down out of sight behind an empty stall. I stuck my face up to the boards and shut one eye, trying to peer out through a crack.

"See if anyone's home," said a rough, deep voice that made me shiver just to hear it. "I'll check the barn for feed."

I could see plain enough that there were three of them. I suppose they could have been just friendly neighbors. But I doubted it. They were scraggly and mean looking. I couldn't help but be reminded of the men who'd killed our families.

"Look through here," I whispered. "Anybody you know?"

Katie leaned across me and squinted, then leaned back and shook her head.

The next moment we heard the door of the barn creak open, and a shaft of light followed. Then came the dull thud of boots walking slowly across the wood floor. Katie was huddled so close I could feel her whole body shaking. She stuck her head against my chest, and I put my arm around her and stroked her hair. I was afraid she might start crying, but she didn't.

Suddenly the boots stopped. The man was in the middle of the barn, only about twenty feet from us. I could sense him looking around.

"Anybody there?" he called out.

Silence. I wondered if he could hear our hearts pounding.

He stood there for what seemed like forever. Then the boots started walking again. I heard what sounded like oats being scooped out of the bin into a bag, then he went back outside.

I peeked through the crack again. The other man was just walking back from the door of the house.

"Ain't nobody in the house, Jeb," he said.

"Abandoned?" asked the man who had been in the barn. He handed the bag of oats to the third man, who started giving handfuls to their horses.

"Don't look like it. Place's all tidy and a fire's on. Fresh bread's on the table."

The one called Jeb scratched his chin.

"Huh . . . barn looked worked too," he said.

"Might be women here. Wouldn't hurt to look around."

I felt Katie's trembling become even more noticeable.

"I could use a woman, Jeb," he went on. "It's been—"

"Shut up, Hal, you fool! You'll get all the women you want after we find what we're looking for."

"Where are they, then?" asked the other.

"Don't know."

"Out in the fields someplace?"

Jeb shrugged. "From the looks of it, there's folks about."

"Then we'll just wait and kill 'em when they come

back," snarled the other man with a nasty laugh.

"Yeah, and you're a blamed idiot. Ain't you had your fill of killin'? We don't need a price on our heads. 'Sides, we'll never find him if we kill his kin. If this is his sister's place, then she's likely to know something."

"Maybe not, Jeb. We ain't found a trace of him in months. He likely never even made it back this far."

"What else we gonna do? We'll just feed our horses and rest up a spell. When they come back, we'll just be real friendly and ask if they can put us up for a couple a nights. We'll do our nosing around and get a lead on Ward and the dough. Now go inside and rustle us up some grub. I'll unhitch the horses."

They're sure to find us sooner or later, I thought. We had to do something.

"Come with me," I whispered real quiet to Katie.

Slowly I got to my feet, took her hand, and led her toward the back of the barn. If we could get out the back door and make a dash for the woods, we might be able to get away without being seen.

I opened the door slowly. It was a good thing it didn't make much noise. Nobody was in sight. The three men were all still on the other side between the barn and the back of the house, or maybe they'd gone into the house by now.

"Can you run with me?" I whispered.

Katie nodded.

"Then let's go."

We got outside. I closed the door behind us carefully, then we took off side by side. The first trees were maybe fifty yards away. We had to climb over one rail fence, which we did. By then we could have been seen from the kitchen if anyone had been looking out the window. But I heard nothing behind us.

We ran as fast as we could, and in another thirty feet we were in the trees. Katie stopped and fell to the ground.

"Not yet, Miss Katie," I said, "we've gotta get farther. They can still see us from here."

I gave her a hand and pulled her to her feet. We ran a little more and when we couldn't see any of the plantation buildings I finally began to feel safe.

We stopped to catch our breath. After half a minute I started walking again.

"Where are we going?" asked Katie.

"We're gonna try to get back to the house," I said. "We'll have to keep in the woods. But if we walk all the way around to the other side, we'll come toward the front of the house without them seeing us."

"Why?" said Katie. "What are we going to do?"

"I ain't sure yet," I muttered. "I'm workin' on it."

"What did that man mean about finding the dough?" asked Katie. "Was he talking about our bread?"

"No, Miss Katie—dough's money. It sounds like they're looking for money."

"But we don't have any."

"We might, Miss Katie," I said.

"What do you mean?"

"Your uncle's gold. Didn't you hear? They said they were trying to find Ward."

Her eyes got wide again.

"But it doesn't sound like they think the gold is here," I said. "—Come on."

There was no time to think about gold now. I had to figure out a way to get rid of the men . . . and keep ourselves alive!

We crept through the woods, making a great big wide circle back toward the house. I half hoped we'd imagined the whole thing or that we'd get back and find the men gone. But after what had happened already to both of us, I don't guess there was much sense in thinking like that. This predicament was happening all right, just like everything else we'd been through.

And sure enough, the men were still there. I saw the three horses tied up in back. I ducked back into the woods and we kept going.

As we sneaked through the trees and bushes, I gradually came up with a plan in my head. A pretty crazy one, I reckon, but then what else could we do?

When the coast was clear and I hoped the men weren't looking, we scurried toward the front of the house on the opposite side from the barn and kitchen where the three had gone in, making our way closer and hiding behind each of the big oaks until we were approaching the big white front entryway.

34

M ISS KATIE," I WHISPERED. WE WERE AT THE FRONT of the house and ducked down low against the wall. "—You know where your daddy's guns are? In that cabinet in the hall between the living room and the parlor?"

Katie nodded, her eyes getting big again. "What do you want with my daddy's guns, Mayme?" she said.

"We're gonna try to scare those men away."

"How?"

"I'll tell you when the time comes. What I want you to do first is sneak around the side of the house, there toward the kitchen wall. Keep under the windows. When you get to the corner, get some rocks and throw them at their horses."

"Rocks—what for?"

"To startle 'em. When they run outside to see what's wrong, I'll dash in and grab us two guns."

"But, Mayme—"

"You can do it, Miss Katie. Don't be scared."

"I *am* scared!"

"Nothing will happen to you."

"What if something happens to *you!*"

"Nothing's gonna happen to me neither. I'll be in and out of there quicker'n you can snap your fingers."

"What should I do after I throw the rocks?"

"Keep hidden around the corner. The minute you see the men coming out the door, get back to the front of the house and out there into the woods and past the oaks where we just were. I'll meet you there."

"I can't do it, Mayme. What if they hear—what if they come after me?"

"You'll be clear on the other side of the house while they're out tryin' to figure out what spooked their horses."

She wasn't none too pleased about the arrangement. But she finally nodded and said she'd try. And I've got to hand it to her, she held up her end bravely enough.

I helped her get going off along the side of the house between the white columns, making sure she hunched down under the windows. Then I crept up onto the front porch. I waited.

When I heard a rock thud on the ground in back and a horse start to whinny, I opened the door a crack to listen. I heard chairs scraping back from the table and booted feet going out the door.

I darted inside, into the hallway by the parlor and to the cabinet. I fumbled to get it open, took out a rifle and a shotgun, then grabbed a bunch of shells, stuffed them in my dress pocket, and hurried out the way I'd come.

The second I was out the door I saw Katie across the field ahead of me from one oak to the next, holding her dress up and running like a jackrabbit.

I took off after her, but not as fast since I was lugging the guns. I was glad the house was between the horses and us. Every second I was afraid of shouts or a shot behind me. But neither happened. We made it to the woods and ducked down out of sight again. Both of us were gasping for air.

"You did right fine, Miss Katie," I said between breaths.

"I was scared," she panted.

"So was I. But look—I got the guns."

"What are we going to do with them?" she wanted to know.

"We're gonna shoot 'em."

"Shoot the three men!"

"No, silly, just shoot the guns off. Scare 'em."

"I never held a gun in my life."

"Ain't nothing to it. Except it gives a little kick on your shoulder."

"What do you mean, a kick?"

"It just knocks you back a bit. You have to lean into it so it doesn't knock you on your rump."

"But how're we going to scare them?"

"By making them think a whole bunch of men are shooting at 'em. Now, come with me. I'll show you what to do."

"Oh, Mayme. I'm afraid. What if I do it wrong?" she moaned.

I pulled her to her feet, and handed her a gun, which she took in her hands like it was going to explode any second.

"You'll do fine, Miss Katie. We've gotta get your house back. We don't want them to stay here, do we? They might stay forever if we don't do something."

"How do you know how to shoot a gun, Mayme?" she asked again, like she couldn't help herself.

" 'Cause I watch and listen," I said as patiently as I could. "I've seen white men with guns, and I listened to our own men talk about them. The master used to take my grandpapa hunting with him, and grandpapa talked about it. Grandpapa kept one of the master's guns in our cabin, and I used to watch him clean it. But I've never shot a gun in my life either. I just figure it can't be too hard."

I carefully looked over at the shotgun I held, then the rifle in Katie's hands.

Katie just stood there staring at me like she did when she was all worked up about something. It wasn't the easiest thing in the world to think clearly when some-body was staring straight into your face from about a foot away. But I did my best.

I figured Katie'd be safest right here, at the edge of the woods, far away from the house. I leaned the shotgun against a tree so I could show her how to use the rifle.

"You're gonna shoot this one, Miss Katie," I said. "It ain't got the kick of a shotgun, but you still gotta lean forward and hold on tight."

She looked terrified.

"Now here's how you load it," I explained. "We'll load it right now—here's the shells. I'll leave this handful with you. Just put them on the ground beside you. Here . . . take a few shells. . . ."

I made her take some and load them into the gun herself so she'd know how.

"You might need to load and shoot real fast," I said.

"Why, Mayme?"

"If something goes wrong—if they come after you, or if something happens to me—"

"Mayme!"

"Miss Katie!" I said sternly, forgetting myself, "now you gotta grow up real fast. We're in a dangerous pickle, and if those men come after you, you might have to shoot at them. That's just the way it is. It can't be helped. Just stay hiding here in the trees so they can't see who you are, then shoot, reload the gun, and keep shooting toward the house.—Let me think for a minute."

I was trying to remember when we'd been looking at the men from inside the barn.

"Do you recollect if those men were wearing gun-belts?"

"I don't remember. I don't think I saw any guns." Katie's voice trembled.

"Me neither. We'll hope not anyway."

"What are you going to do, Mayme?"

"I ain't sure. But first I'm gonna go back to the barn with the shotgun. Once we start shooting, we don't know what they'll do. I'll just have to do what comes to my mind. But if something happens to me, you just keep shooting."

"Oh, Mayme . . . I'm so scared!"

"Me too. But we've gotta try to get rid of those men. Now here's what I want you to do.—You see the back of the barn past the house?"

She nodded.

"I'm gonna sneak back there. First I'll see if I can swipe their rifles off their horses. I don't know if I'll be able to. Then I'll go back around and into the barn. When you see me go inside the back door where we came out, you count to three hundred like this—" and I counted slowly to give her the rhythm—"and then you start shooting. It doesn't matter where you shoot. Just aim up in the air over the fields there someplace. I just want them to hear it and come running outside. When they do, then I'll start shooting from inside the barn. You load the rifle up again as fast as you can and empty it again. But this time aim sort of in the direction of the house, over the top of the house or something. But not toward the barn!"

"How do you aim it?"

"Just point it, that's all, and look down the barrel. And remember, when you pull the trigger the first time, hold on real tight. After that, you'll get the hang of it and it'll get easier."

There was no time for her to practice. She'd have to learn how to shoot a gun by doing it, and I hoped she didn't shoot herself—or me. If we hadn't been so desperate, I would have started laughing at the look on her face.

"I'm going now, Miss Katie. Can you do it?"

"I'll . . . I'll try, Mayme."

With Katie in place, I crept back toward the barn. As confident as I'd tried to sound for her sake, I was mighty scared myself. I didn't more than half think it would work. But if it didn't, and they came after us, especially if they tried to hurt Katie, well then I reckon I was ready to shoot at them for real—even try to kill them if I had to. But I hoped it wouldn't come to that.

I got to the barn all right without seeing or hearing anybody. The three were probably in the kitchen eating that fresh bread we'd just made.

I put the shotgun down against the wall of the barn and inched my way along the far outside wall, then ducked down low and walked in a crouch toward their horses from behind. There were all three rifles sticking out of the rifle pouches beside the saddles! Once I got close I started talking to the horses real quiet-like to keep them from getting jumpy, then rubbed their noses and necks. They moved around and snorted a little, but didn't raise too big a fuss.

I pulled out the rifle closest to me. The horse got a little skittish, but I kept stroking its side and whispering to it. Then I walked around and got the next rifle and put it under my arm with the other one.

But the third horse didn't like the idea of me walking up so close. It turned and kept moving its hind end away, and I couldn't get to the gun.

"Take it easy, you!" I whispered. "I don't mean you no harm . . . come here, calm down."

I scratched under its long chin for a few seconds with my free hand, but it was still acting nervous. I was getting nervous too. This was taking way too long! I had no idea where Katie might be right now in her count.

Finally I just ran forward before the horse could move again and grabbed the gun and yanked it out.

The horse gave a little whinny and stomped around. But by then I was running back for the barn as fast as I could with the three guns.

I hurried behind the wall and stopped to listen. I still didn't hear anything from the house. The horses calmed down again. I was pretty sure no one had seen me.

I caught my breath, then picked up the shotgun where I'd left it and snuck back along the wall, around to the back of the barn, and then inside. I hoped Katie had been watching.

I made my way over to the house side and peeped out one of the barn windows. If I could just shoot at them and get them scared without them coming after me . . . but I guess I wouldn't know that until I saw what they did. I leaned the four guns against the wall, then got out two shells and started to load the shotgun.

Then came an explosion of gunfire—Katie must've hit three hundred!

I had to get ready quick.

I figured I'd better just stay by this open window. I slammed the lever down and lifted the gun.

Another shot sounded from the woods, then a third. I heard yelling from inside the house. A few seconds later the men came running out, looking frantically around.

Three more shots fired.

Katie'd figured out the rifle just fine! Now she would have to reload, and it was my turn.

One of the men was looking toward the woods

where Katie was hiding. And he *wasn't* wearing a pistol around his waist! None of them were.

"Get the rifles!" he shouted to the others. All three started running toward the horses.

I reached the barrel of the shotgun up and over the window ledge, aimed in the direction of the men's running feet, and pulled the first trigger.

The kick nearly knocked my shoulder in half, and its roar was so loud I thought it would split my head open.

A big blast of dust flew up and one of the men swore real loud. I don't know if some of the buckshot got him in the leg or if he was just surprised at the sudden sound.

"Our guns is gone!" one of them shouted.

I figured I'd better keep them on the run. I emptied the second barrel as close to their feet as I could get.

From the yells and hollering I heard when the echo died away, I could tell I must have aimed just a little too high. One of them sounded like he was in pain.

Behind me, there came Katie's gun again . . . one shot, two . . . three. Then I heard a window shatter with the next shot.

Miss Katie! I said. *What are you doing! Don't shoot at the house!*

I had no idea if the men's rifles were loaded. But rather than risking the time to reload the shotgun, I grabbed the closest rifle and started firing in the air over their heads.

It was loaded all right!

Now with Katie and me firing together, shots were

exploding every other second. The three men hurried to untie their horses and leap onto their mounts.

"Let's get outta here!"

"What about our guns, Jeb?"

"You want to go back and try to find them, fine by me, Hal! But I ain't ready to get myself shot for no gun."

They spurred their horses around as I threw down the rifle and quickly fumbled with the shotgun, opened the chambers, and reloaded.

The three galloped off along the road west with dust and dirt flying up behind them. They were far enough away by now that I didn't figure it could hurt anything, so I let both barrels loose straight at them.

Whether any buckshot got that far, I don't know. But they didn't slow down and a minute later were out of sight.

I ran out the back door of the barn waving both my hands in the air.

"Miss Katie . . . Katie!" I shouted toward the woods. "They're gone! You can come out now!"

I ran across the field. She crept out from between the trees and just stood there looking at me.

"Miss Katie," I called again, "they're gone!"

Now she took some steps toward me, then started running. We met in the field in a great big hug, laughing and crying all at once.

"We whipped our weight in wild cats, didn't we?" I yelled. "I got their guns and we scared 'em off."

She was shaking with excitement and fear and exhilaration all at once.

"Did you count clear to three hundred?" I asked when we'd settled a bit.

"I was so nervous, I lost track when I tried to count," she said.

"And you shot out one of the windows!"

"I was trying to aim over the roof."

We laughed again.

"Well, no matter," I said as we walked over to pick up her daddy's rifle. "It worked out all right. But we'd better get back inside with all the guns, and be ready in case they come back."

"What will we do then, Mayme?" asked Katie, getting serious again. "We won't be able to scare them off like that a second time."

"I don't know, Miss Katie. We'll just have to hope they don't come back until we get something figured out."

I Make a Decision

35

B
ACK IN THE HOUSE, WE WERE BOTH FRIGHTENED
and excited for the rest of the day. We'd scared
them off once, but like Katie said, we might not be so
lucky again.

The rest of the day passed without any sign of
trouble.

My mind was still racing into the night, and I could
hardly sleep for listening to the sounds outside.
Crickets and bullfrogs and every once in a while a
coyote and a few strange noises I didn't recognize
kept me awake half the night.

I kept the rifle in bed with me this time instead of the
Bible.

All kinds of things were running through my mind,
such as that we ought to go to that neighbor's house
the next day and ask for his help. Then I remembered
that I was black and he was white, and what was I
thinking.

I didn't know what to do. All I knew was that we
were in a fix even worse than before.

The next day we were both still spooked, jumping at
every sound, listening, looking out the windows, worrying that we were going to see those riders coming up
the road.

After all that had happened, I got to thinking harder than ever. Katie was going to get found out, that much I was sure of, and it wouldn't likely take much longer.

Somebody with mischief in mind would come here eventually, someone we couldn't just scare away with a few gunshots. We were only a few miles from Greens Crossing. Sooner or later those men would come back. Or one of Katie's uncles would come calling and claim Katie and Rosewood for their own.

Before long, *somebody* was going to get mighty curious about why no one had heard from Mr. and Mrs. Clairborne in so long. If we were found like this, a fifteen-year-old white girl and a colored girl living alone together on a great big plantation, I couldn't think of anything but bad things that would be the result.

Sometime between when I went to bed and woke up the next morning, I realized I'd reached a decision.

The next morning during breakfast I said to Katie, "You don't want to go live with your aunt or your uncles?"

"No," she said.

"Then there ain't nothing else, Miss Katie, except one of those homes for kids that ain't got a ma or pa."

"An orphanage?" she said, sounding like she was going to cry.

"Something like that," I nodded.

She looked at me in shock.

"Oh, I could never do that!" she said. "They beat the

children when they're bad. I've read about work houses in books—they're awful—"

"You might have to go to someplace like that, Miss Katie, if you don't decide something else."

I could tell she still didn't understand. I was starting to get exasperated.

"Don't you know, Miss Katie—they're going to find out! I've been telling you all along that I have to leave sometime, and soon. And if you don't *do* something, you're gonna have to go to your aunt or one of your uncles or some kindly person around here . . . or else to an orphanage."

Katie was silent.

"You can't wait any longer. It's time you did something. People are gonna start asking what's going on. They're gonna wonder if there's a colored in the woodpile, and if they ask too many questions they may *find* one too—me! So what I want you to do, Miss Katie," I went on, "is either go to that neighbor man who came by—he seemed like a decent enough sort—or else go into town and tell somebody what happened and that you need help."

"But, Mayme—"

"You're in danger, Miss Katie. We saw a whole dose of danger yesterday. You need somebody to take care of you. Somebody who can do a better job of it than me."

"But . . . who am I going to tell about everything?"

"Somebody you trust—the banker, that neighbor man, that general store lady . . . any of them would help you, Miss Katie."

"I can't, Mayme."

"What about a minister?"

"There's Reverend Hall, but I hardly know him."

"That don't matter. Do you trust him? Could you talk to him?"

Suddenly a determined look came over her face.

"I won't," she said. "You can't make me do it!"

"You got to, Miss Katie."

"What if I don't?" she said, sounding like a little girl telling her mother she wasn't going to obey.

"Miss Katie," I said. "I'm leaving."

The words hung there in the air between us.

Gradually Katie got the most stunned look on her face I'd ever seen. She just stared back at me like she didn't believe what she'd heard. Slowly her face got red and her lower lip quivered. Then she started to cry.

"It's for your own good," I went on. "There ain't nothing else to be done. Something bad is going to happen to you. I've got to make you do this, Miss Katie."

"But . . . but, Mayme—"

"Now, you go to that banker. You can trust him. Or go to that Mrs. Hammond or the reverend or *somebody* and you tell them about your ma and pa and that you're alone."

"What about you?" she said while tears poured down her cheeks.

"By then I'll be gone, Miss Katie." I could hardly get the words past the lump in my throat. But they had to be said.

"Gone—?" she repeated, like I'd slapped her in the face.

"It's for the best. I'll find some other coloreds, like I said, and they'll take care of me."

"But what if something bad happens to *you*, Mayme?" she asked as she started to cry again. "I'll be so worried about you."

"You just take care of yourself, Miss Katie, and don't bother your head about me. I'll be fine."

She sat quietly, and I couldn't exactly read her expression.

"But, Mayme," she said finally, "I don't see why you can't just . . . just stay. Why can't you be my slave at Rosewood?"

"Because, Miss Katie, that ain't the way it works. I'm *not* your slave. I belong to Master McSimmons, at least I once did. I can't be anything but bought, sold, or a runaway. And right now, that's what I am—a runaway."

"But there wasn't anybody there when we went back to your house."

"All we saw was the colored town. For all we know, everything's still the same at the big house. If Master McSimmons is dead, maybe that changes things a mite. But I still belong to *somebody*, just like this plantation of your mama and daddy probably belongs to somebody else now. Everything belongs to somebody, and that's what slaves are—property that somebody owns. And now that I'm a runaway, I don't see much else for me to do but either go back to the McSimmons plantation, or try to make my way up North."

Katie listened and again she got quiet.

"What if I won't do it?" she said after a while.

"Miss Katie, you *got* to let your kin know!"

It was silent a long time. I think she finally realized that I was dead serious.

"When . . . when will you go, Mayme?" she finally asked. Her voice was soft.

"Tomorrow, Miss Katie," I replied. "I'm leaving tomorrow."

I didn't like the thought of being out on my own either. But it had to be done. The decision had been made.

"Where, Mayme . . . where will you go?"

"I don't know, Miss Katie. It's best for you if you don't know where I am. That way you can't get into trouble for knowing too much. If people ask about that colored girl who was around, just tell 'em I came for a while and then left and that you don't know where I am."

"But . . . but, Mayme . . . will I ever see you again?"

She looked at me with those big eyes, and their sad expression nearly broke my heart. It was all I could do not to give in and say I'd stay just a while longer. I swallowed hard and took a deep breath.

"I'll try to come back sometime and see you," I answered. "Whether you're here or someplace else, or up North with your aunt, whoever's here—or that lady at the store—they'll know where you are. I'll come back when it's safe, maybe when we're older. We'll stay friends, Miss Katie."

She listened with more great big tears running down

her cheeks, then turned and walked up to her room.

I followed and listened from the bottom of the stairs. I was sure she was lying on her bed. It hurt to hear her sobs, but I knew I had to go.

There was no use putting it off any longer.

GOOD-BYE TO ROSEWOOD

36

K ATIE KEPT MOSTLY TO HER ROOM FOR THE REST OF the day. I heard crying coming from behind her closed door a few times, but I knew that as long as I stayed around, Katie wouldn't do anything to change the situation.

I had washed the tattered old dress I'd had on when I first arrived, and I'd put it away just in case the day ever came when I'd need it again.

It looked like that day was finally here.

I lay in Katie's brother's bed that night, thinking about all that had happened and the decision I'd made.

My heart was breaking, more for Katie I think than myself. I couldn't tell for sure what she was thinking, or if she realized how serious I was. And I had about a dozen second thoughts myself. But every time I'd come back to the conclusion it was the right thing to do.

This would be my last night here in this nice soft bed. I'd been at Rosewood long enough to get used to the comfort, but it was time for me to go back to being a colored girl again. If Katie was going to get found out, it'd be better for us both if I wasn't around. I couldn't pretend that I belonged in her white world any longer.

Gradually I dozed off to sleep.

I don't know how much sleep Katie got that night, but I sure didn't get too much. What time I woke up I don't know, but it was still dark. I knew more time in bed was useless.

I realized that in a way we'd already said our good-byes. There wasn't much sense in prolonging the sorrow of parting any more than I had to. It would only make things worse. So I might as well just get up and leave.

As I got out of bed, my eyes started to burn, but I tried to ignore them. I tiptoed across the floor, got out my old dress, and quietly changed into it.

A minute or two later I tiptoed toward the stairs holding Mama's Bible and a few other things that Katie had given me wrapped up in a bundle. I noticed one of the guns still propped against the wall where I'd put it in case the three men returned. At least Katie knew how to use it now, but hopefully she wouldn't have to.

I continued on downstairs, then lit the lantern in the kitchen and sat down to write Katie a short note. It took me longer than I expected, because it was none too easy. Then I got myself a little food, blew out the lantern, opened the door, and crept out into the darkness.

There was just enough moon to see my way past the barn. I heard a few noises inside, but this was no time to let the animals distract me from what I had to do. Then I started walking down the road through the darkness.

My eyes stung with tears and my heart ached as I got farther away. But I couldn't let myself look behind me.

My mind went back to everything that had happened, my first few days here, how Katie had been when I first found her, how we'd slowly put the place back together and gradually started getting to know each other, then become friends. I thought of all we had managed to do together. It was only a short time, but it seemed like a year. The day before I'd thrown out some pretty high-sounding ideas about us getting together later and keeping in touch with each other. But now I wondered if I ever would see her again.

Good-bye, Rosewood. Good-bye, Miss Katie. . . .

Then the tears finally began to pour out of my eyes. I hadn't said those words out loud, but they kept going over and over in my head. Between the darkness and the tears, I couldn't see where I was going and nearly fell over a rock. But the hurt inside was worse than a stubbed toe.

Where *was* I going? I thought to myself. I took a deep breath and tried to force myself to think.

There wasn't much use going into Greens

Crossing. And the colored village at the McSimmons place had been deserted. I had only about a day's worth of food, no money, and only the clothes I was wearing.

I reckoned maybe, just like the old song said, I had nobody but the angels to watch over me now. Since I hadn't really figured out where I was going yet, I wasn't in any hurry and was walking pretty slow. Even though I had no plan in my mind, I found myself moving toward town and the direction of the McSimmons plantation. After a while it started to get light. Every so often I'd hear a horse or wagon in the distance, and I'd hide off to the side of the road in the woods until they were past.

Gradually the sun came up and it got warmer. It must have been several hours later, after hiding from another wagon, I was lying in the grass out of sight. I felt real tired. I started to get drowsy and pretty soon fell asleep.

37

B ACK AT ROSEWOOD, THREE OR FOUR HOURS AFTER
I'd left, Katie woke up suddenly.

It was early in the morning and the sun was just
coming up. Some sound had awakened her, and her
first thought was that the troublemakers had come
back.

"Mayme . . . Mayme!" she called frantically as she
fumbled into her clothes. She ran into her brother's
room still calling my name.

Just about the time she figured out I wasn't there, a
bloodcurdling scream came from the direction of the
barn. By then Katie was plenty scared. She hoped I
knew about whatever was going on and was already
outside.

She hurried downstairs and into the kitchen, whispering my name just in case it was those men. Then
she saw my note on the kitchen table.

She read it, started crying when she realized I was
saying good-bye and that I was gone. Whatever her
thoughts were, they were interrupted by another howl
from the barn.

Still crying, but without stopping to think, she ran
back upstairs, grabbed the gun, and came down again.
She went through the kitchen, opened the door as qui-

etly as she could, and tiptoed outside.

She wiped away her tears and glanced toward the hen house, but the chickens were quiet as they could be. So she started walking in the direction of the barn.

When she was about halfway there, suddenly the morning air filled with another scream. It sent a shiver all through her. For a moment she forgot about me, and fear took over. The scream had come from the barn for certain. But it sure didn't sound like any fox.

Katie kept going, gun at her shoulder now.

Maybe it was something like a bobcat or a small mountain lion! Trembling, she put her finger gently on the trigger, ready to shoot if some creature flew out after her. I wish I could have seen her right then—scared to death, eyes big and still red from crying over my note, and holding up a rifle nearly as long as she was tall.

She inched the barn door open and crept through it into the darkness. As her eyes adjusted, the dim light showed a black face with two large eyes. For a brief second she thought it was me.

In relief she lowered the gun. But then she heard a voice she knew *wasn't* mine.

"Don' shoot me, don' shoot me!" it yelled. "I's jest a girl!"

That was what she was all right, a black girl crouched down in a pile of straw about ten feet away, her face full of terror.

When Katie realized she was nothing but a runaway

slave girl, her emotions started going all over the place. She was heartbroken all over again that it wasn't me and suddenly got mad.

"What are you doing here?" she shouted. "You likely scared the wits out of me. I could have shot you!"

Katie was probably more irritated at me for leaving than she was with the girl. But the girl was there and Katie took it out on her.

"Please don' hurt me! I thought dose men was gwine ter kill me. I jes' had ter git away."

"How long've you been around?" she said. "You've been stealing stuff from our house!"

"Jus a litter bread. I had ter git away. I was hungry an' I couldn't—"

She cried out again and writhed around in pain. All of a sudden Katie realized why.

"You're . . . you're going to have a baby!" cried Katie, her eyes opening wide in shock.

"I'm doin' mo' den jes' gwine ter hab one . . . I'm habin' der baby *now!*"

"Now! You can't have it now . . . not here."

"I can't help it—it's comin'!"

I've got to hand it to her, in the midst of all she was going through, Katie didn't waste time trying to decide what to do.

She turned and ran out of the barn and straight for the house. She dropped the gun on the porch, ran upstairs, and a minute later was hurrying back to the barn with a blanket. As soon as she had made the girl a little more comfortable, she hurried to the stables

231

and started saddling a horse as fast as she could.

"What's you doin' . . . where you goin'?" babbled the girl.

"I'm going to try to find help," said Katie.

"But you can't tell no one I'm here . . . dey can't find me!"

"Just lie still till I get back," said Katie as she opened the big door and led the horse outside. "Maybe if I hurry I can catch up with the only person who can help us."

With the girl crying and calling out behind her, Katie scrambled up on the horse and galloped away.

ANOTHER MEETING

38

I DON'T KNOW HOW LONG I SLEPT BY THE SIDE OF THE road. It might have been an hour or two. I was tired and hadn't had much sleep the night before.

I woke up slowly, sort of still half dreaming. At first I forgot where I was. Then I remembered—I'd left Rosewood and said good-bye to Katie. A huge feeling of sadness rolled over me again, not knowing if I ever would see her or if I ever would have a place that felt so much like home as Rosewood did.

Where is my home? I thought to myself as I lay there in the warm grass. *Where do I belong?*

I didn't have any family left in the whole world.

Only Katie. Was she my family now? There wasn't anybody else. . . .

In the midst of my drowsy thoughts, I heard a voice calling my name.

At first I thought I must still be asleep and dreaming. Then it came again, closer and a little louder.

"Mayme! Mayme!"

With my name I also heard the sound of hoofbeats.

Now I knew I was wide-awake. I crouched down lower so I wouldn't be seen.

"Mayme . . . Mayme, where are you? Please . . . Mayme!"

Hearing Katie's voice, a hundred thoughts whirled through my brain. What was she doing out here? She must have read my note and come after me. I couldn't let her talk me into going back! I had to keep her from seeing me!

I lay there for a few seconds, battling inside about what to do. But as I heard Katie calling again, it wasn't like anything I'd heard from her before. Her voice sounded desperate, pleading. She was riding fast too. She was almost even with where I was.

My eyes filled with tears. I tried to blink them away and stay down, but it was no use. I *couldn't* let her go by.

Slowly I stood up from the grass and walked out of the trees toward the road.

"Mayme!" Katie nearly shrieked with joy as she saw me. She jumped down off the horse and ran to me.

"Mayme . . . you've got to come back right away!"

She sounded so urgent, we didn't hug or say anything about my note or my leaving.

"Come, hurry," she said again, "—get up on the horse!"

She didn't give me the chance to argue as she climbed back into the saddle and reached for my hand.

"But what's—" I began.

"Hurry, Mayme—there's a girl in the barn who's going to have a baby. You've got to help me!"

Before I knew it I was up on the back of the horse with her, trying as best I could to keep hold of my stuff. The minute I was hanging on around her waist, Katie kicked the horse, and we galloped back the way we'd come.

We got back to Rosewood faster than I ever thought Katie could ride a horse. With the wind in our faces and the sound of the horse's hooves pounding along the dirt road, we could hardly hear to say anything to each other. About all I was able to figure out from Katie yelling back at me was how she'd gotten up and heard a scream, then found some colored girl hiding in the barn who she said was about to have a baby. By the time Katie got that out, we had just about covered the three or four miles back to Rosewood.

Katie reined in the horse. "Hurry, Mayme," she yelled. "In the barn. I'll tie up the horse—you go look."

We both jumped down and I ran into the barn.

There was the girl just like Katie said. Sure enough, she was having a baby!

"Praise Jezus!" exclaimed the girl when she saw me.

"I'm fixin' ter hab a baby!"

A look of pain filled her face. She winced and squeezed her eyes shut tight and cried out.

"Lawd almighty, girl—I can see that!" I said. "You's as plump as a ripe watermelon!"

Her face grimaced something dreadful. "Hit's comin' an' I don' know what ter do. I'm scared!"

"Well, why are you trying to have it here!" I shot back. I don't reckon I was thinking too clearly. "Where you bound to—you gotta get to your own kin."

"I ain't got none no mo, least none dat I can go to. Dey made me go away. Dey's fixin' ter kill me."

"What are you talking about? Nobody's gonna kill you."

"Din't you hear all dat shootin' a couple days ago?"

"That was us. Besides, those men weren't after you. I tell you, you can't stay here."

Another scream came and she collapsed back into the straw. For a second I thought she had passed out.

All at once her eyes shot open again.

"Hit's comin', hit's comin' . . . I'm afraid!"

"But you *can't* have a baby here!" I said again.

"Go git da mammy!"

"There ain't no mammy here, I tell you."

A loud groan followed. Then, "Git yo own mama den," she pleaded in a forlorn wail. "Git somebody ter help me!"

"There ain't nobody here to help you!"

Just as the words were out of my mouth, I heard Katie come into the barn.

"Oh no! Da missus . . . she's gwine scold me again!" cried the girl, looking up at Katie. "I'm done fer now! Please, missus . . . don' hurt me!"

Another terrible scream erupted out of her mouth.

"Miss Katie," I practically yelled over the sound, "this fool nigger's going to have a baby!"

"That's what I've been telling you, Mayme," said Katie, hurrying toward us.

"Missus . . . please don' hurt me!" cried the girl.

"Just be quiet," said Katie, stooping down beside her. "I'm not going to hurt you."

"I'm sorry I done took yer bread," she went on hysterically, "an' I know hit's yer barn an'—"

"It's all right," said Katie, stroking her forehead and trying to calm her.

". . . I know I ain't got no right ter be here, but I din't hab no place ter go, an' dey's after me an' I'm feared dat—"

"Be quiet!" Katie yelled, putting a hand over the girl's mouth. "Listen to us, and we'll try to help you."

For a second she stared back at Katie with great big eyes. All at once it seemed to dawn on her what Katie had said.

"Praise ter Jezus!" she cried. "Thank you, missus! I don' know what ter do . . . an' I'm scared."

Katie took her hand.

"Please, missus . . . please help me! Hit hurts fearsome bad an'—"

She winced in pain and cried out again.

"Mayme," said Katie, looking back to where I was standing, "we've got to do something."

"Thank you, missus!" she said, squeezing Katie's hand for dear life. "Praise Jezus—I knew yo'd help me! But, missus . . . I don' know—"

"Just be quiet," said Katie. "Try to relax and don't talk. Mayme, what should we do?"

"I don't know," I said. "All I know is they always boil water for birthing."

"What for?"

"I don't know."

"No sense in us doing it, then," said Katie. "But we should get some more blankets for her, and a pillow."

"I'll go fetch them, and maybe some towels," I said. "They're always using towels."

I tore out of the barn toward the house. There'd been plenty of birthings in the colored village, and people were always giving orders and fetching stuff. But without my mama or one of the older women around, the thought scared me. I don't suppose I was acting altogether full-witted yet, but it had all happened so fast. I hardly noticed that Katie seemed calmer than me, and was telling me what to do.

As I got to the kitchen door, another shriek sounded behind me. Even while the sound of it was dying away, Katie's voice followed.

"Hurry, Mayme!" she yelled.

B Y THE TIME I GOT BACK TO THE BARN LUGGING another blanket, a few towels, a pillow, and a pail of water, I'd heard two more shrieks out of the girl. Whatever was going to happen, there wasn't anybody else to help us. Even though we were just girls, it looked like we were going to have to be women now.

Katie was still kneeling beside the girl, talking to her and trying to make her comfortable.

"Her name's Emma, Mayme," Katie told me. "She's been hiding here in the barn for a couple of days. She's nearly famished from hunger.—Here, Emma . . . here's another blanket, we're going to put it under you.— Mayme, help me tuck the blanket under so she can lie on it."

Katie leaned the girl up a little as we got the blanket down onto the straw and past her shoulders and back, then helped her lean back and forth till we could pull it the rest of the way and get her lying on the blanket instead of straw. Then Katie put the pillow under her head.

She wasn't hollering so much now, with Katie holding her hand and talking gently to her. But her forehead and cheeks were drenched in sweat, and I can't say she smelled any too good. Every so often she'd cry out a little and twist up her face in pain.

"Dat feels good," she said as she leaned her head back onto the pillow. "Thank yer, missus—ye're bein' so kind ter me eben dough I dun stole yer bread."

"Don't worry about the bread, Emma," said Katie. "And I'm not a missus—I'm just a girl like you. My mama was the mistress, but she's . . . she's not here. My name's Katie. And we'll get you something more to eat real soon.—Mayme, dip a towel in some water so we can wash her face."

"Jezus, bless yer soul, Miz Katie . . . ye're so good—"

She cried out and grabbed at Katie's hand.

"Laws, it hurts, Miz Katie! I can't help it . . . I'm so scared!"

"Just lie still, Emma," Katie said gently. "Everything is going to be fine. You don't mind if I pull up your dress a little, do you, Emma?"

"No, Miz Katie . . ."

She was grimacing in pain every few seconds by now it seemed, and each time it came over her, she leaned forward and her whole body tensed up. But Katie kept holding her hand and trying to calm her.

"Get a towel, Mayme," said Katie as she drew Emma's dress up. "Put it down there by her so the baby—"

Emma screamed again, louder and longer than before.

Katie helped her get her underthings off, and then I saw why the girl was yelling so often. Her knees were raised, and all at once I saw the top of a tiny little dark

239

head trying to push its way out from inside her.

"There it is!" I yelled. "It's coming!"

The next second Katie was at my side. "Take her hand, Mayme—talk to her," she said. "I'll help with the baby.—One or two more times, Emma. You're doing good . . . it's almost over."

"Laws . . . owwww. . . ."

"Here comes your baby, Emma," said Katie, reaching to help guide the little head the rest of the way out.

Emma shrieked again. "I can't . . . ow—Miz Katie!"

"It's coming, Emma!"

Emma bent forward and grimaced and pushed. For a couple of seconds the barn was completely silent. Then suddenly I heard a swoosh, and a second or two later the tiny cry of a baby.

"Emma, you did it!" Katie cried, and as I looked up, her face was smiling like I'd never seen it before. Emma collapsed back against the pillow with her eyes closed, still sweating and crying and breathing heavily. But it was only for a second. The crying of the baby brought her eyes open again, and a faint smile came to her parched lips.

"It's a little boy, Emma!" said Katie. "—Mayme, help me . . . get that other towel . . . help me dry him off."

I did what she said, hardly knowing what to think. How on earth did Katie know how to do all this!

As I was helping her I noticed something about the baby that seemed mighty peculiar. But I didn't have the chance to think about it right then.

"Go back into the house, Mayme," said Katie in the middle of my thoughts. "Get my mama's scissors from the sewing room. We have to cut the cord. And a bottle of alcohol from the pantry . . . hurry."

When I came back, I stared almost bewildered while Katie splashed alcohol on the scissors, then cut the cord by the knot she'd tied and dabbed it with some more alcohol and wiped away the blood.

Katie wrapped the baby in one of the clean towels and gently held him out to Emma.

"Here's your baby boy, Emma," she said. "Do you want to hold him?"

Emma reached out her arms to take him, then just stared at the little thing she was holding, studying his tiny fingers and little ears and even the little toenails.

"Thank you, Miz Katie . . . ye're been so good ter me!"

"What do you want to call him?" Katie asked.

"Da chil's name be William," I heard Emma answer softly.

Katie covered her up with the end of the blanket and a clean towel. Emma was exhausted. It looked nice and peaceful, the little baby at his mother's breast, and in less than two minutes both of them were asleep.

But there was still something bothering me.

Katie gathered up the dirty towels and pail of water and walked toward the barn door.

I just kept staring at Emma and the baby for a few seconds, hardly believing what I was seeing, then I followed Katie out of the barn.

A DIFFERENCE

40

WE HARDLY HAD A MINUTE TO OURSELVES FOR THE rest of the day. What with Katie fussing over Emma and the baby, if I hadn't known better I'd have thought Katie *was* a missus, and that Emma was her own little girl!

Katie was younger than either me or Emma, and here she was acting like mistress to the whole place. I don't know why it bothered me. I'd never minded anything she said to me, but seeing her being so nice to a dimwit like Emma stuck in my craw, and I couldn't get rid of it.

We had left them sleeping there in the barn and walked back toward the house. Katie's sleeves were rolled up and she was carrying two bloody towels. Her face was glowing with satisfaction. I wasn't saying much, and by now we'd been around each other long enough to know what the other's frame of mind was.

"What's eating you, Mayme?" said Katie.

"Can't you tell?" I said.

"Tell what?" she asked.

"That baby's father's a white man."

"How do you know?"

"Look at him. You can tell by the color of his skin."

"His hair's curly and dark."

"That doesn't matter," I said. "Emma's as black as a sky with no moon, but that child's light as can be. I've seen a heap of colored babies, and that little boy's the son of a white man."

Katie shrugged as she put the towels down by the washtub in the yard. Then she washed her hands. "I don't see what difference that makes," she finally said.

"It makes all the difference," I shot back. Probably my voice sounded a little irritable because that's what I was feeling.

"Why?" asked Katie, with a little edge creeping into her voice too.

"Because—because it means she lay with a white man, and that ain't right," I answered. "She ain't married to whoever that boy's father is, and it's wrong. It ain't nothing but a little bastard son of a white man."

Katie thought a second.

"I suppose you're right," she said slowly. "About somebody doing wrong. But that's not the baby's fault, and it's not right for *you* to call it such a name. The baby can't help what color it is or how it got here. You're not prejudiced against whites, are you, Mayme?"

"How can you say that?"

"I don't know—why would his light skin bother you? You're not near as black as Emma either."

"That's different. There's all shades of colored folks."

"Then why are you upset about little William's color?"

"That's another thing—that's a white name," I said, ignoring her question. "Why would she give it a white name? And so quick-like. There wasn't a second's hesitation—'Da chil's name be William,'" I said, and I reckon I was a little sarcastic as I repeated Emma's words. "I don't like it."

"What's come over you, Mayme?" Katie asked. "This isn't like you.—Well, no matter," she said without giving me the chance to answer, "we've got to try to get her inside."

"Miss Katie," I exclaimed, "you're not thinking of putting her in one of your beds!"

"She can't stay in the barn. We have to feed her and get her a comfortable place to rest up."

"But . . . I figured you'd make her go back to her own kin."

"Maybe later," said Katie. "But she can't stay in the barn. And besides, we don't have any idea who her kin even are."

"She's just a runaway slave girl who's birthed a white man's baby."

Katie stopped and looked at me in a way she'd never done before.

"Mayme," she said, and I could tell she was more than a little annoyed with me, "we have to take care of her. And we are *going* to. So help me get a bed ready, and then help me get her inside."

I didn't argue any more about it. Katie's voice made it clear enough that there wasn't anything further for me to say on the matter. With all that had just happened, I didn't know what I was going to do now. Just when I'd gotten up the gumption to leave . . . now this. I couldn't very well walk out on Katie now, with a dimwit like Emma and a little newborn on her hands. And yet . . . I didn't think I ought to stay either. I'd made up my mind the day before, and I didn't want to go back on it. I reckon my pride was getting the better of me.

A couple of hours later, after she'd had a good sleep, we half carried Emma inside. She was skinny as a rail and wasn't too heavy and we managed to get her into the house. Katie arranged a bed for Emma on a sofa in the parlor. She said it would be easier for us to take care of her there.

Katie busied herself warming some soup, then sat beside the sofa feeding Emma with a spoon for the next hour. The girl was so weak after what she'd been through that she could hardly sit up or talk. But Katie sat beside her and spoke softly to her and fed her and gave her milk.

Every once in a while, when I'd walk by the room, I'd hear Emma talking a little crazy, like she was half awake or half asleep, which she probably was. The baby cried a little, but not too often.

I was still stewing inside, I think as much from having my own plans turned upside down as from anything else. But I had a feeling that if Katie let her stay around, Emma was going to get her into even more trouble than she was already in.

And likely me too. . . .

THE ARGUMENT

41

K ATIE CAME INTO THE KITCHEN AFTER BOTH EMMA and the baby were sleeping again, carrying the empty bowl and cup.

"When are you going to make her leave?" I asked.

"Leave?" said Katie, putting the things in the basin. "She can't leave. She's so exhausted she can't even stand up right now. She'll be in bed for a week."

"A week!" I exclaimed. "She can't stay here that long. She's going to get you into some bad kind of fix before that. Didn't you hear her say somebody was after her?"

"No," Katie answered slowly.

"Well, she did."

"It doesn't matter. They won't find her here."

"What makes you think that?"

"Why would they look for her here?"

"Somebody could have followed her. What if they have dogs—?"

"We'll hide her."

"Miss Katie! What if the baby starts crying?"

"It doesn't matter," said Katie with that determined voice she'd been using lately. "I'm *not* going to make her leave."

"Well, I don't like it," I insisted. "She's just a thick-headed guttersnipe that's got no right to put you in danger like this."

"Are you really so concerned about *me,* Mayme? Why don't you like her?"

"I just don't," I said. "She's just a dumb colored that got herself knocked up by a white man."

"What's come over you, Mayme?" Katie asked. "Are you so ornery all of a sudden because somebody else needs help now instead of you?"

"You never gave me no help!" I shot back. "It was me that helped you!"

"You're right," said Katie. "I did need your help. I'd have likely died without your help. But now someone else needs help, and I don't know why you're too stubborn to see it. Why won't you help Emma the same as you helped me?"

"It ain't the same."

"What's different about it?"

"It's just different, that's all."

"You know what I think, Mayme," said Katie, and her eyes flashed, "I think you are all mixed up right now. You don't like the thought of me helping someone, especially a colored girl. What if she were a white girl who needed us, Mayme? I think you're jealous of Emma—"

"You think I'm jealous of *her!*" I practically yelled. "She ain't worth it!" I turned around to stare out the kitchen window.

"Well, she's worth something to me!" said Katie at my back, and it was as close to yelling at me as she'd ever come. "She's all alone and her baby's helpless, and she's just about as helpless herself, poor thing. So I'm going to help her whether you like it or not. I don't know anything about taking care of a baby because I never had younger brothers and sisters like you did. I'm sure you know more about it than I do. But if you won't help, I guess I'll just have to learn. And I will too, because she needs me."

She paused and glanced over at my note where it was still lying on the kitchen table.

"So you might as well just leave again," she said, "if you're so determined to go."

"Maybe I will," I said, "just like I said I would."

"Then go ahead!" said Katie in an angry voice. Her face was red again. I guess I'd riled her up pretty good. "But I'm staying here, just like I said too. And Emma and her baby are welcome to stay with me as long as they like!"

"You'd rather have her than me!" I blurted out, knowing even as the words passed my lips how dumb they sounded.

"I wouldn't *rather* have anybody. I don't love you any less, Mayme—"

I couldn't help looking away again. I hadn't expected her to say something like that right in the middle of an argument. Suddenly my eyes stung with hot tears. The words tore me apart.

"—There's plenty of love in my heart to go around," Katie continued softly. "I'd hoped you had the same kind of love in yours. But if I can give some of the love that's in me to Emma too, then maybe I'm supposed to. Maybe that's why she wound up here. When you first came, you and I both needed help, and we helped each other. You're right, you helped me a lot more than I helped you. Maybe that's why I've got to help Emma now."

The kitchen got real quiet. We just stood there looking at each other, both of our faces full of emotion. I reckon I'd dug myself in too deep a hole to climb out of without eating a heap more crow than I wanted to right then. Maybe my pride had got the best of me, and when that happens a body doesn't think too straight or make good decisions.

"Well, I sure as shootin' ain't gonna stick around and wait for that fool to get us in a fix," I finally said. "She'll be the death of us both if she's found here. The day's going to come as sure as sin when somebody comes after her and maybe kills her, and us at the same time."

"Well, I'm not going to make her leave, Mayme," said Katie.

Just then the baby cried out from the parlor. Then came Emma's voice.

"Missus . . . Miz Katie . . . der baby's cryin'. . . ."

For a second or two more Katie's eyes stared into mine. I knew she was pleading with me to come to my senses.

Then she turned and hurried into the parlor.

LEAVING AGAIN

42

I STOOD IN THE KITCHEN FOR ABOUT A MINUTE AFTER Katie'd left.

Finally I picked up the note I'd written early that same morning before it was light.

Dear Katie, I read.

There ain't no good way to say good-bye, so I'm leaving before daylight so we don't have to go through the pain of it. Only one last thing I want to say—and that is that you're the best friend I could ever have in the world. I'll never forget you. I love you, Katie.

Mayme

Tears were already in my eyes before I finished reading it. They were sure more pleasant words than the ones we'd just fired back and forth at each other.

It wasn't much of a way to say good-bye, but I didn't want to have to try to say it again, especially with Katie mad at me.

I set the note back down on the table and slowly walked outside. My Bible and bundle of things were still in the barn. I walked across the yard, through the door, and found them where I'd dropped them earlier. I carried them out and stood by the pump, holding them in my hands and trying to make some sense of all the thoughts and emotions swirling around inside me. Then I set out walking.

A minute later I was on my way down the road again just like I had been earlier. It was so quiet. Even the baby'd stopped crying. It seemed like it took forever for me to get down the road a hundred yards. Tears were coming down my face because I knew Katie wouldn't come riding after me this time, and I knew I couldn't look back.

On I walked, one slow step after another, hating myself for leaving, still thinking I had no choice, though my brain was pretty mixed up by now.

Then again came a familiar voice. I wanted to think I was dreaming again, like I'd thought earlier. But I knew it was no dream.

"Mayme!" Katie called behind me.

I stopped.

"Mayme . . . please don't go!"

Slowly I turned around. There was Katie standing next to the porch.

Before I realized what I was doing, I was running toward her. Then she started running toward me. I dropped the things I was holding . . . and I saw Katie open her arms . . . and all of a sudden we were in each other's arms crying like a couple of babies.

We didn't do anything for a while but just stand there sobbing on each other's shoulders.

"I'm sorry for the things I said, or if I hurt you,"

Katie said finally. "I didn't mean to."

"You didn't," I said. "I was wrong to think what I did. You've been better to me than I deserve. I know you care about me."

"I do, Mayme. You're the best friend I've ever had."

"You too, Katie. I was thinking earlier, when I left this morning, that you were my family now. I don't know how I could leave you. But it just don't seem—"

"Oh, Mayme!" she cried, and she put her hand over my mouth to stop me from saying anything more about my worries. "My heart was breaking in two to see you walk away down the road. I didn't know what to do for the longest time. I just stood watching your back and crying. I don't know what's going to become of us, or what we're going to do. But let's not worry about it just now. All I know is that I couldn't let you leave again."

THE DARING SCHEME

43

THAT NIGHT, AFTER WE HAD ALL EATEN AND EMMA and baby William were settled down for a spell—though he would probably wake up hungry again in another hour or two—Katie and I sat on the bed in what had been my room and had a long talk. We were both pretty sober after hearing Emma's story of how she had come to Rosewood.

Once Katie had heard what Emma had been through, and the danger she was still in, she was more determined than ever not to make Emma leave anytime soon, at least until she and William were healthy and strong. Beyond that we didn't say too much about the future. Neither of us wanted to bring it up again, because I was still unsure what to do myself, and I think Katie knew it.

We didn't actually resolve anything. Katie was just happy that I had decided to stay for one more night and was content not to worry about how I'd feel later. And I reckon that about sums up how I felt myself. I didn't know what I'd do or what was the right thing to do.

Finally we said good-night and Katie went back to her room. I turned out my lamp and pretty soon was sound asleep.

Suddenly in the middle of the night, I woke up.

Katie was calling my name.

"Mayme . . . Mayme!"

Terrified, I jumped out of bed. My first thought was that the men we'd scared off with the guns were back.

I fumbled in the darkness to throw something around me and hurried out into the hallway. Before I could reach her room, Katie nearly knocked me over running toward mine.

"Mayme . . . Mayme!" she said, her voice an urgent whisper.

"What is it, Miss Katie! What's wrong?"

"Nothing's wrong," she said. "I've had the most wonderful idea! Come into my room and I'll tell you."

I followed her, not knowing what to make of it. I was still a little shaky from waking up so fast.

"Get into bed with me, Mayme," she said as she struck a match to turn on her lamp. My heart was finally beating normally again.

We sat there leaning against the pillows for a bit.

"You said it yourself, Mayme," she said by and by. "We're in trouble if anyone finds us alone. So that's what made me realize what we need to do—we've just got to make sure no one finds out we're here alone."

I nodded. It was just what I'd been trying to tell her all along.

"Don't you see—we'll make it look like we're *not* alone!" she went on. "No one will know Mama and Papa aren't still here!"

Her eyes were wide and expectant, like she was waiting for me to jump up out of the bed and dance around or something. But I just kept sitting there staring back at her.

"Isn't that what we've already been doing?" I asked.

"But you said we couldn't *keep* doing it without getting discovered."

"I reckon so," I said. "That's why I decided to leave, because sooner or later we were gonna get found out, or one of your uncles was gonna come and claim Rosewood and take you away."

"But why couldn't we *keep* doing it?" asked Katie. "We can make it so believable that no one ever finds out! Not my uncles or anyone in town . . . or anyone!"

"But . . . *how?*" I asked.

"I don't know, just have things look like normal," said Katie. "Do it even better than we have up till now—make the plantation look like everything it's supposed to be. We can pretend you're one of Rosewood's slaves. Remember Mr. Thurston and Mrs. Hammond? They didn't guess we were alone."

I thought about it, trying to get my mind around what she was suggesting.

"I'm going to do it, Mayme," Katie went on, more serious now. "I'm going to because I have to, for Emma's sake, to keep her safe. But maybe even after she's gone. I don't want to go to live anywhere else. I'm just a girl, like you said, but why can't I make Rosewood mine? I'm sure Mama and Papa would want me to have it. And I'm going to! I want you to stay, Mayme. And I hope you do. But whether you do or not, I've got to get Rosewood up and running again. Don't you see—I've got to. I've got to for

Emma . . . and for me too!"

"But I still don't see *how* you can keep going on like we've been doing," I said. "We're already starting to run out of things. And what will you do when winter comes or if something happens and you get sick? And how would you buy things? What would you do if you went into town and people asked about your mama? What are you gonna do when you run out of sugar and salt and matches and other things like that you gotta buy? You don't have any money, do you?"

"No," said Katie. "But that doesn't matter, Mayme. I still think I could do it . . . especially with your help. I think we could pull the wool over people's eyes enough so that they wouldn't bother us."

Little by little her unbelievable, incredible idea began to dawn on me.

"So you actually think," I said, "that you can keep doing like we've been . . . keep doing it till you get old enough so that the plantation's really yours—honey-fuggle everybody into thinking the others are still here—your mama and daddy and the slaves and everyone?"

"Yes . . . yes, Mayme—that's it!" laughed Katie, excited again.

It was silent for another minute.

"By the horn spoons, Miss Katie," I added, shaking my head, "that's some daring idea all right."

"I know what I'm saying could be dangerous," said Katie. "But I'd rather be in danger and us be able to stay together and me be able to stay here."

"But . . . but do you really *want* me to stay?" I asked.

"I'm the daughter of slaves. You're the daughter of a white man. Even if you could get away with it and gum people into thinking you weren't alone—"

"Mayme," she interrupted me, tears suddenly replacing her laughter, "I *want* you to stay."

Her words made me feel like crying too. It got real quiet for a minute.

"Maybe it wouldn't work forever, like you say," said Katie after a bit. "All I know is that right now I don't want to go live anywhere else. I want to stay right here and take care of Emma and baby William."

"But . . . but like I said before when you had to talk to that Mr. Thurston," I said, "you wouldn't lie and tell people your folks are still alive, would you? You once said you couldn't do that."

Katie thought for a minute.

"Lying's wrong—I know that. But I remember my mama once telling me when the war came that sometimes people had to do hard things they didn't need to do at other times. So maybe I could do it, if it would protect us and Rosewood," she said. "Me not having to go to one of my uncles or to an orphanage and keeping you here and being able to help Emma."

"I sure don't know about all this, Miss Katie," I said. "but . . . but it'd sure be some pumpkins if you *could* do like you're saying!"

Katie thought a minute.

"I'd try not to lie," she said thoughtfully. "I guess if I had to, to keep whoever's after Emma from finding her and hurting her, well, I don't know . . . maybe I'd have to. But I hope not."

Just Me and God

44

A FTER TALKING A LITTLE MORE, WE WENT BACK TO
our own rooms again. I don't know about Katie,
whether she'd had to get up in the night to see to
Emma and William, but I slept sound right through
until it had begun to get light.

Even though yesterday had been a long day and
Katie and I had been up late the night before, I came
instantly wide-awake. The minute I sat up in bed I had
the sense that somebody had called my name and
that's what had woken me up. But it was completely
silent. I don't know what time it was, but it was early
and there wasn't a sound coming from anywhere else
in the house.

What could have made me wake up so suddenly?

I lay there for a few minutes, and then had the
feeling that I should get up.

As I got dressed and slowly tiptoed from the room
and downstairs, the most peculiar sensation came
over me that it was God who had awakened me. The
idea made me feel funny—like God *knew* me, knew
my name, and was now quietly saying it—*Mary
Ann Jukes, get up . . . come outside. I want to talk to
you.*

Did God really talk to people like that?

Did God talk to people . . . like *me?*

I was a nobody, a black, a slave with no family, with nothing to call my own. I reckon I was about as insignificant a person as there could be on the face of the earth.

Would God really pay attention to someone like me? And why would He want to talk to me?

I didn't have the answers to all those questions, but I figured I ought to do what He said and find out what it was all about.

I went out of the house and started walking. Before I knew it, I was walking toward Katie's special place in the woods. It was so quiet and still in the morning. The sun wasn't even quite up yet.

Not only was it quiet out in the morning, it was quiet inside me too—quiet and still and peaceful. For the first time in a long while, I wasn't worried about what to do or where to go. Maybe thinking about God does that to you—quiets you down inside and makes you less fretful. I was a practical kind of person that usually had to have everything all figured out. But on this morning I wasn't worried about anything except right then, and being where I was supposed to be at that moment. And it was a good feeling too.

Slowly I walked along through the woods, looking around me as the birds woke up too and began to sing.

Just as I reached Katie's little meadow, I saw a deer about forty feet in front of me drinking from the stream. It pulled its head up and looked at me. It didn't seem afraid, and we just stood looking at each other for a few long seconds. Then the deer slowly walked away and disappeared in the woods.

I went the rest of the way into the meadow and sat down on the rock where Katie sat to write her poems and think.

I sat there for the longest time, just thinking about all that had happened. Then I remembered that God had woken me up—maybe called my name—though I still didn't know why.

I wasn't too experienced at praying. I'd really only prayed that one time a couple of weeks before when I'd been reading in my mama's Bible. But I figured if ever there was a time when I needed to pray, maybe that time was now.

"God," I said, talking softly, though it sounded a little funny to hear my own voice in the middle of that meadow when the morning was so quiet, "I don't know why you woke me up and wanted me to come out here, but if you've got something to say, I reckon I'm listening. You must know that I've been a mite confused about what Katie and I should do, and especially about what I ought to do. I thought I should leave and I even tried to twice. But it just hasn't seemed to work out, and now I don't know what to do. . . ."

I stopped and took a deep breath.

Again it was silent a long time. Gradually I began to get the sense like I had before that God was talking. But His voice was so still and quiet that I couldn't hardly make out what He was trying to say.

How were you supposed to hear God's voice

anyway? Maybe you had to get so still yourself that His voice kind of stole inside you in the midst of the quiet.

So I closed my eyes and tried to relax and shut out all my own thoughts and ideas to see if maybe I could make out what God was saying.

I sat for a while with my eyes closed, just breathing in and out and being still . . . and waiting.

Then slowly a thought came into my mind and then eight words followed it. I didn't really *hear* them, but it was *like* hearing them. This is what the words said— *Ask me what I want you to do.*

"Was that you, God?" I asked out loud. "Was that you saying that?"

Again, someone repeated the words and I heard them in my mind. *Ask me what I want you to do.*

Then I realized that ever since I'd been trying to decide what to do and whether or not to leave Rosewood, I'd never once talked to God about it. All I'd done was try to figure out *myself* what to do.

I wondered if there might be a difference between what you wanted to do *yourself,* even if you thought it was right, and what *God* wanted you to do.

And how else could you find out what He wanted except by asking Him? Was that why He'd woken me up and gotten me to get up and come outside, so I'd learn how to ask *Him* instead of doing what I thought I ought to do? Was that the prayer He was trying to teach me to pray, how to ask *Him* what to do?

If that was it, I thought, it was a whole new way of looking at things, a whole new way of looking at life.

I'd always done whatever I figured I ought to do. That was the kind of person I was. I just did what I thought was best.

Maybe that wasn't how it was supposed to be after you'd opened up your heart to God. Maybe you were *supposed* to ask somebody else, and who else would that be but God?

I sat for a long time in silence. I didn't get any more feelings that God was saying anything. Maybe He'd said all He had to say.

If that was true, then I reckoned it was time I did what He'd told me to do—ask Him.

God had had His say. Now it was my turn. I don't suppose God keeps talking to someone who's not paying attention to what He says. If you want Him to keep talking to you, I guess you've got to keep your half of the conversation going, and right now I figured that my half of the conversation was to do what He'd told me.

"All right, God," I said finally, "I suppose I've been trying all this time to figure out myself what to do. So I'm ready to listen to you now. I'm asking, like I think you told me, what you want me to do. Even if it's different than what I think, I'll do what you tell me. So, God, what do you want me to do?"

There wasn't anything more to say. I suppose when you ask God what He wants from you, that's about the best prayer you can pray, and so I stopped.

The quietness only lasted a little while.

Suddenly more words came to me so clear there was no doubt about them. *I want you to stay,* they said.

I sat up straight.

"God, was that you answering my prayer?" I asked.

I want you to stay, came the answer again.

Slowly a smile spread over my face.

I don't know if I mentioned before how I'd sometimes been curious whether God was black or white. But it didn't matter—God had spoken to me!

God had listened to the prayer of a black slave girl called Mayme Jukes and had answered her. He cared enough about that girl called *Mayme* to tell her what He wanted her to do!

That's pretty nice, I thought. All you had to do to find out what God wanted was to ask Him! What could be simpler? I'd have to start asking Him what He wanted me to do more often. It wasn't until I was older that I grasped all the implications of what I'd done. But it was a good start and got me thinking about God in new ways.

After a bit I got up. As I came out of the woods and began walking back to the house, the sun was up and I could feel its warmth on my face. That's how I felt inside too—warm and happy because God was looking down at me, and because He knew my name and cared about me, and wanted me to talk to Him and wanted me to do the things He told me.

I think someplace between the woods and the house I knew that a big change had come into my life. In a quiet, peaceful sort of way, I knew I was a different person than I'd been when I'd walked into the meadow and sat down. How could you not be changed when God speaks personally to you—just to *you* and nobody else?

God and I had just had a conversation together. That may seem like a simple enough thing. But it was a big thing for me—bigger than I know how to say.

God and I had talked to each other!

That's an amazing thing when you stop and think about it. God made the world and everything in it, and they say He loves everybody and is taking care of everything in the whole world all at the same time. So for God to love *me* enough, in the middle of all that, to talk to me and help me and tell me what to do— wow, that's about the most amazing thing in the world!

Somehow I knew I was going to have lots of conversations with Him after that day. And I knew that when He had something He wanted me to do, He'd tell me.

And whatever it was, I was going to do my best to do it.

MAKING PLANS

45

W HEN I GOT BACK TO THE HOUSE, KATIE WAS UP
and busy with Emma and William. For the rest
of the morning there never seemed to be a good time
to talk to her. I guess I was pretty quiet for the rest of
the day and mostly kept to myself. After what had
happened at Katie's special place in the woods, I
didn't know what to tell her. How do you tell someone
that you've been talking to God? I had no idea what
she might think.

But I was happy inside. I knew that God loved me
and cared about me. I guess those were things I'd
always known. But it was different now—I knew
them in my heart. And I felt warm and at peace inside,
at peace with God, at peace with my future, and at
peace with myself.

It wasn't till Emma and William were again asleep
for the night that I finally got up the courage to tell
Katie about that morning in the woods. Maybe
courage is the wrong word. But sometimes it's hard to
talk about personal things even to the people you love
the most. At least for me it's hard.

When we were alone together, Katie must have
noticed that I was being quiet. I could see she was nervous. She probably thought I was fixing to leave

265

again. So I told her about getting up early and going out to her special place in the woods and about praying that God would tell me what I should do.

"And what did He tell you?" asked Katie, like it was nothing out of the ordinary to talk to God.

"I'm pretty sure He said that He wants me to stay," I answered.

"Oh, Mayme!" Katie exclaimed. "Do you mean it—does that mean you're going to stay?"

"I reckon it does, Miss Katie," I said. "I think I'm supposed to . . . I think God wants me to."

"And you'll help me get the plantation running like everything's normal!"

"I reckon so," I nodded with a smile.

Katie was practically jumping up and down on her bed with delight, and I couldn't help but laugh to see her so happy.

"What will we do first, Mayme?" she said. "We'll have to start making changes right away. I know we can do it!"

"But do you realize what it will mean?" I said, my practical side coming back now that the decision had been made. "We will have to get the plantation working again, crops and animals, and go into town and buy things and do whatever your mama and her men were doing before, but without anyone ever noticing anything's different."

"Yes . . . yes—I can do it, Mayme!"

"What if we ain't strong enough for something? What would we do when people came to visit and wanted to see your mama?"

"Just like we did before, Mayme!"

"But sooner or later people are going to get more and more suspicious," I went on. "And what will we do about the crops? Right now all the corn and cotton that your mama's slaves planted earlier, it's all growing. What will we do with it come fall? How are two young girls like us, especially if we're trying to take care of Emma and William at the same time, how are *we* gonna run a plantation, Miss Katie? It ain't just the fields and crops, it's the smoking and the gardens and butchering and the fencing and buying things."

"But we don't need to do *everything,* Mayme," insisted Katie. It seemed nothing could dampen her enthusiasm. "There's only four of us, and all we have to do is make sure we have enough to eat. And one of them's going to need only his mother's milk for a while."

"Maybe that's all we need to get by," I said. "But we'd have to do a lot more to make the place look alive enough so that folks don't get suspicious."

"We fooled those three men, didn't we?"

Slowly I started grinning.

"Just think," I said, "—two girls, one colored and one white—putting some kind of hornswoggle like this over on everybody!"

Katie laughed with delight.

"Yes . . . yes! We'll start tomorrow, Mayme," she said. "Let's at least see if we can figure out what to do."

"All right," I said, smiling. "It's worth thinking about some more."

"Oh, thank you, Mayme!"

She jumped over and gave me a kiss on the cheek.

"All right, then," I said, climbing into the bed, "if we're gonna get to planning out this scheme of yours of trying to run a plantation, Miss Katie, I reckon we'd better get some sleep in what time we got left before morning."

She got into bed beside me. It was the first time we'd slept together in a while and it made me feel warm inside.

"Good night, Miss Katie," I said.

"Good night."

She paused and looked over at me.

"Thank you for staying, Mayme," she said. "I love you."

Had she really just said what I thought I'd heard?

I felt my eyes getting all misty.

"I love you too, Miss Katie," I said.

When I woke up in the morning, the sun was already coming through the window. Whatever little William had been up to during the night, I'd slept right through it. And Katie wasn't next to me any longer.

I didn't know how long I'd slept in, but there was definitely a change about the place already!

I heard baby noises downstairs, with Emma talking to her little boy in a soft, high voice and sounding better than she had all the day before. She must have been getting some of her strength back. I wondered if it had occurred to her yet, like it had the first time for me, that she was sleeping in a white man's home. We'd found out that she'd been a house slave before running away, so maybe she was a little more used to nice things than a field slave like me had been.

Downstairs in the kitchen I heard Katie singing! I couldn't tell if it was some piece from that man Mozart or one of the colored songs I'd taught her. But one thing was certain—it sounded happy.

I dressed and went downstairs.

She had a nice fire going and was busy at the cook stove.

"Good morning, Miss Katie," I said as I walked in.

"Good morning, Mayme!"

"What are you doing?" I asked.

"I thought, if I'm going to be doing what my mama does—did—around here," she said, "that I better get up early and start to work. I think Emma's going to be able to eat some regular food today, and I'm hungry too!"

I rolled up my sleeves and walked across the floor to help her with the breakfast makings.

"Yep," I said, "I reckon now our work really begins."

It was quiet a few seconds.

"Oh, Mayme," Katie exclaimed, setting down the big wooden spoon in her hand and looking at me with a wonderful smile. "It feels like there's hope again that things are going to be all right!"

"Maybe you're right," I nodded. "I reckon there's someone watching over us after all."

Epilogue

A WEEK LATER A WAGON HEADED INTO GREENS Crossing. Two young women sat on the seat. The white girl who was driving the team wore a pale green-and-white frock, gloves and bonnet, and looked every bit the aristocratic young lady. The other, who was taller and plainly attired as a slave, wore a simple blue chambray work dress and straw hat. But whatever the differences in the color of their skin, they seemed to be having a good time, singing and laughing as they neared the town.

The wagon was far larger than what was needed for transportation alone. The two clearly had come with the intent of picking up supplies for one of the nearby plantations.

No one in Greens Crossing suspected the secret that this black girl and white girl shared—especially the secret back in the house at Rosewood.

They had to find out if they could keep it that way. If they could get past the watchful eye of the town busybody, Mrs. Elfrida Hammond at the general store and post office, they could fool anyone.

That would be their first stop.

Center Point Publishing
600 Brooks Road ● PO Box 1
Thorndike ME 04986-0001 USA

(207) 568-3717

US & Canada:
1 800 929-9108